Dear Readers,

I still remember the first time I read Donald Goines, the godfather of street lit. He was the first to write books about characters I could identify with. To some, the stories may have been aggressive, overly stylized, and even dangerous. But there was an honesty there—a realness. I made a vow that if I wrote a book or got into the publishing game, I would try the same one-two punch—that of a Daddy Cool or Black Gangster.

Last year, my memoir, *From Pieces to Weight,* marked the beginning. Now I'm rounding up some of the top writers, same way I rounded up some of the top rappers in the game, to form **G-Unit** and take this series to the top of the literary world. The stories in the **G-Unit** series are the kinds of dramas me and my crew have been dealing with our whole lives: death, deceit, double-crosses, ultimate loyalty, and total betrayal. It's about our life on the streets, and no one knows it better than us. Not to mention, when it comes to delivering authentic gritty urban stories of the high and low life, our audience expects the best.

That's what we're going to deliver, starting with **Nikki Turner,** bestselling author of *A Hustler's Wife* and *The Glamorous Life;* **Noire,** bestselling author of *G-Spot* and *Thug-A-Licious;* and finally **K. Elliott,** author of *Street Fame.*

You know, I don't do anything halfway, and we're going to take this street lit thing to a whole other level. Are you ready?

G Unit
Books

DEATH BEFORE DISHONOR

A 50 Cent
and Nikki Turner
original

POCKET BOOKS, a division of Simon & Schuster, Inc.
1230 Avenue of the Americas, New York, NY 10020

ISBN-13:978-0-7394-7885-1

Manufactured in the United States of America

This book is dedicated to
the last of a dying breed,
those who still live by and will die by
three words . . .
DEATH BEFORE DISHONOR

Acknowledgments

First and foremost, I have to thank my God, who has given me so many opportunities to excel in this game and to keep my cup running over with blessing after blessing.

To my constant motivation, my two children, Timmond and Kennisha, you two bring so much sunshine to my life! My nanny, Ms. Carol, I never thought anyone could take care of my children as my grandmother did, but I thank you for caring for them while I am writing and chasing my dream! I thank you for the bottom of my heart! Craig, my best friend, time and time again, for never leaving me for dead no matter the crazy circumstances! My sister/friend, Kia—keep reaching for dreams, they do come true! Brenda Thomas, you keep me grounded.

50 Cent, it is such a HUGE honor that of all the people in this industry, you knew to come to me to headsail your fleet of ships, G-Unit Books! You have truly changed the game, bringing the best of both worlds together. Thanks for putting this project on cruise control, trusting me to cre-

atively navigate the launching of this fleet—a mastermind you are! You have no idea how much you have changed my life.

Lauren, thanks for keeping an open mind when it came to the editing of this book. K. Elliott, we've grown to be such great friends throughout this journey. You keep me laughing.

My editor Melody Guy at Random House, which is my literary home, for allowing me to step away to the G-Unit condo long enough to blaze this book, and return back to continue my commitments to you. Thank you for seeing the BIG picture.

Marc, my agent, time and time again for always amazing me with the deals you bring to me. Keep them coming!

Special thanks to: Kermit Gresham (I see your name in lights), and Vamps and Vixens—you are so talented and I thank you for only being a phone call away! Terria Coleman, thank you for working wonders with my hair at the last minute when my stylist was sick. Thomas, you keep my eyebrows clean as the Board of Health and working with my crazy schedule!

To every Nikki Turner reader and 50 Cent fan, we thank you for your constant love and support as we make history together!

There are three means of communication:

Telegram,

telephone,

and . . .

tell a bitch.

—50 Cent and Nikki Turner

1

The
Best
Orgasm

unni sat at her mahogany desk with a big smile plastered on her face, squirming, feeling the moisture between her legs. She was getting wet as she counted all of the men who had run up through her place of business that day and given her so much pleasure. There was Alex, Ben, Drew, Abe, Tom, Grant and George. Grant was one of her favorites, except she had to see him twice to reach the climax that Ben always brought her to. Ben was the best of the best, a certified big hat. Just looking eye to eye with him made her explode like no other orgasm she had ever had in her life.

Sunni didn't notice her best friend, Cher, standing in the doorway, watching her about to climax.

"Damn, chick," Cher said. "If dick ain't never made

you cum in the past year, I swear those benjamins have."

Sunni didn't respond until she finished counting her salon's night deposit. She came out of her trance when the money was sealed in the plastic pouch the bank provided for business owners.

"Girl, be quiet," was her delayed reaction. "After all that good dick I done had, who would have thought that I'd be saying, 'fuck dem niggas, I want the money'?"

"Damn, that's what an empty, broken heart can do to you."

Just then Beatrice, one of the stylists that Sunni had fired earlier that day, entered her office. "Excuse me, can I talk to you?" Beatrice asked.

"What is it?" Sunni snapped, wondering why Beatrice was back up in her shop. "Is it about my money?"

Beatrice ignored the question. The last thing she wanted to do was get into a verbal battle with Sunni, so she calmly said, "I really need to talk to you."

"So talk," Sunni said. She could cut people up with her tongue and had no problem drawing her sword.

"I know I haven't paid you, but I need to get my supplies from you before I can give you any money. I need my stuff to make money," Beatrice said minkly, not wanting to set Sunni off.

DEATH BEFORE DISHONOR

"Until you pay me my money, you can't get nothing from me," Sunni shot back. "You worked in my shop for weeks—shit, over a month—and never paid me a dime booth rent. And you think that I'ma let you get your stuff back?"

"How am I going to make money and pay you if you don't give me my stuff back?"

"Sell some pussy. I don't give a damn. All I care about is my money."

Beatrice was hot, but what could she do? She shouldn't have left her supplies out in the open. "I'ma get you your money, don't you worry," Beatrice said as she turned and walked away.

"You're going to have to," Sunni said in a singsong of victory.

Ta-Ta, another stylist, walked in as Beatrice was leaving. "I say take it out that ho's ass if she don't want to pay." Ta-Ta specialized in boof-to-the-roof ghetto hairstyles. Bottles of hair gel and bags of weave were all that surrounded her station, located in the very back room of the shop.

Since the twenty-four-hour salon catered to all people, Sunni gave Ta-Ta the evening shifts. She didn't come in until after 6:00 P.M. and usually worked until the wee hours of the morning laying hair down. When Ta-Ta came into the shop, so did eighty-five percent of the gossip, which she sprayed through her teeth like a can of oil sheen.

"If all my workers were like you, I wouldn't have to be locking up people's shit," Sunni said generously, glancing up at Ta-Ta and her bright orange hair. She was so successful at what she did because she was a product of her own craft. Ghettofabulous was her middle name. And for every track of weave she put in, a piece of gossip came out. That chick worked like a slave and brought a lot of money into Sunni's shop.

Sunni stood up and put her bag of money in her purse, next to her gun. Best believe a soul wasn't going to touch her loot.

"Now make sure that my office door stays locked," Sunni instructed Ta-Ta.

"I don't know why you ever gave that damn Beatrice a job noway," Cher jumped in.

"Everybody deserves a chance. I mean, look at me," Sunni said, raising her arms and looking around her private office in the rear of the salon. A client who happened to be one of the city's hottest interior designers had decorated it. The mahogany furniture accented the tan color on the walls. The black-and-white still photos that graced the walls were framed in mahogany frames on bright yellow mats. The chairs were pale yellow leather with silver legs; the floors a yellow-and-cream checker-board. Sunni had spared no expense once she turned her first profit.

"I feel ya," Ta-Ta said to Sunni with her arms folded, "but she was Scoop's cousin. I'm sorry, any nigga that sends me to the penitentiary, I ain't giving nobody he knows a job. He cost you three years of your life," she said as she blew a bubble.

Sunni focused on her grandmother's picture on the wall above Cher's head and thought about Scoop. Which just pissed her off. The more she thought of Scoop, the angrier she got at Beatrice, who was the next best thing to Scoop to take her anger out on. Which was probably the real reason she had fired her.

"Do you ever think of Scoop?" Cher asked Sunni.

"He sent me to the penitentiary. What the hell you think? Hell, I thought about how I wanted to . . . naw, I try not to think of how I want to kill that bitch-ass nigga!"

Cher could see the emotion on Sunni's face, and she knew that the incident with Scoop wasn't something that Sunni wanted to talk about. So she switched it. "Girl, have you heard from that guy we met at the mall the other day?"

Cher and Sunni carried on with the majority of men

who crossed their paths just like men tried to carry on with women. They would turn him out, and if it was good, they passed his ass on to each other, and talked about him after *Sex and the City* went off. It was real for Sunni like that. She loved getting her pussy licked. If she hadn't witnessed in jail firsthand all the extra drama and emotional abuse that came with lesbian relationships, she would have long found her a woman to kick it with by now. But since bumping coochies and getting her grass cut by another woman wasn't her thing, she decided that she would carry it like a nigga. "Money Over Niggas" was her golden rule. She would get her money right and make cute dudes her boy toys whenever she felt the urge.

The last toy she played with was a guy named Mason. Mason was broke as a broke-dick dog, but, boy, could he lick a clit. He did it so good that Sunni played dude like a quick trick, paying his $99 cell phone bill in return for him giving her best friend some boss head, too. And that fool did it. Just like men did women, Sunni and Cher laughed and talked about him like a dog afterward.

Sunni cut the conversation short. "I've got to get to the bank. I'm tired, hungry and sick of the smell of burnt curling irons."

Lust at First Sight

gave up on that shit a long time ago: love, marriage, the white picket fence. Hah. Sunni laughed out loud as she sat at the red light. After a long, hard, fourteen-hour day, she was good and tired. She had been slaving over customers' hair, enduring not only the heat from the curling irons, but the steamy gossip at the twenty-four-hour beauty salon that she owned and operated. Since her release from the Virginia Correctional Center for Women in Goochland two years ago, her shop had become her life.

While she waited for the light to change, she saw a happy couple crossing the street, strolling with their new baby. The guy looked like such a doting father and the woman was smiling as they shared what looked to be their planned parenthood.

For richer and for poorer, in sickness and in health, ride or die, hold that nigga down, Sunni thought as she chuckled. *Yeah, isn't that just cute? It's sweet now, but what happens when your emotions for that nigga override your intellect? Shit, the last time I tried to stand by a man, be the Bonnie to his Clyde? That motherfucker left me with three years in the penitentiary.* Sunni sat at the light analyzing the couple with a big platinum chip on her shoulder that might as well have been engraved with the words "fuck dem niggas."

Sunni's last *so-called* man, and first real boyfriend, Scoop, promised her the world and everything in it. But that nigga couldn't even give her his word, let alone the whole fuckin' world. And in Sunni's eyes a man whose word wasn't good didn't deserve a place in the world nohow.

As she watched the happy couple strolling down the street, anger and envy started to simmer in her mind. She hadn't had any kind of man in her life since she got out of jail, besides the boy toys that she and Cher played with. She didn't want to think about her past another second, so she redirected her attention to the driver of the black Hummer next to her. He was on his cell phone talking, but his eyes shifted over to hers. Neither of them could look away. Something about his thick eyelashes captivated her, and the unspoken chemistry between them was undeniable. Although he looked like he was into an intense conversation with one of his soldiers, there was no doubt that Sunni had his undivided attention.

"**Much as you listen** to that nigga 2-Pac, you violated the number-one rule," Trill riffed into the phone to his boy, Mont. "Money Over Bitches. It's MOB 'til we die, not 'til our dick gets hard." Trill continued over Mont's respectful laughter, "Pussy over fuckin' money, huh? That's how you do yours?"

"Naw, man, I just overslept, that's all," Mont said in his defense. "I'm about to get up now."

"It's too late now, nigga," Trill spat. "You need to open up a savings and loan if you like to make your own hours, but it ain't no bankers on this team."

Mont just listened. He was wrong, and there was no question about it. But Trill should have been handling his business himself. Just like any boss anywhere in America, any general in any army or any pimp in the streets—when the soldiers are slacking, the general steps up and handles the business. When the hos can't do the job, the pimp goes out and makes the money. And this wasn't different from any hustling nigga on the come-up. One monkey don't stop no show.

Trill was sitting in the truck listening to *Ready to Die*, in deep thought about the game plan. He was angry that even though he was the leader of a major money organization, he had to be reduced to the mule and make this drop. But this was one of the crew's valued customers. Trill was riding with four kilos of hard beige in the stash box. He'd had the stash box installed in his truck three months ago at a rim shop in Atlanta even though he never intended to use the truck for transporting merchandise. Naw, this was a straight floss mobile, a black-on-black, spanking clean Hummer with shiny Ashanti rims, but he had the elaborate concealed compartment put in so he could stay close to his assortment of firearms. Getting caught late in the mean, cruddy streets of Richmond, Virginia, was not an option for a major player like Trill; he needed his guns. Richtown had a reputation for leaving blood in the air. Besides, he had more than enough hoopties with state-of-the-art hiding places for transporting narcotics.

He had made rules for his crew months ago. One was: never transport drugs in one of the whips that they flossed in. He made a mental note to start following his own rules.

DEATH BEFORE DISHONOR

While Trill waited to hear what Mont had to say for himself, he maintained eye contact with the fine girl parked next to him at the red light. For a split second he was trying to decide which was cuter: her or her special ordered car, a yellow Cadillac XLR with a chocolate drop-top.

"Man, I be there in fifteen minutes," Mont said. "This ain't your drive. You don't know the area. Let me handle that."

"I ain't got time for you to get your dick back in your pants," Trill said in disgust. "I'ma handle this and get at you tomorrow." He hung up.

His childhood friend had let him down—again. The only time that Mont hadn't let Trill down was when they were fourteen. They had saved each other's lives and vowed that they were in debt to each other, until one or both of them died. That was the only reason Trill halfway tolerated Mont and his inconsistencies.

As he finally broke the stare between him and the girl in the ride next to him, he nodded and gave her a smile. She didn't reciprocate the gesture. The light changed to green, and the mysterious beauty sped off in her XLR in a hurry to get somewhere—probably some big old home in the suburbs.

3

2-High
Speed Chase

As Trill cruised through the little hick town of Ashland, he consciously abided by all the laws. It didn't matter, though, because the sheriff was sure he had hit the lotto when he spotted his mark: a young black male driving a $60,000 truck. The Hummer happened to be Sheriff Bowman Body's dream truck. A truck he could only dream of having with his salary, and he despised the fact that some punk who probably never even finished high school was riding around in it.

Trill could have been wearing a priest's collar, but as far as Bowman Body was concerned, he was a drug dealer and a prime victim of the monthly driving citation quota. Before Trill could think twice, the sheriff's blue lights were bouncing off of his rearview mirror.

"Fuck!" Trill shouted. He beat his hand on the steering wheel as he spat the word out. He quickly looked down and, after making sure that his secret hiding place was secure, then pulled over. He watched from his side mirror as the small, thin-featured sheriff approached the car. His walk was like Forrest Gump but his look was the Terminator, coming to devour.

"License and registration, boy!" the sheriff said with authority as he knocked on the driver's side window.

Trill rolled down the window halfway. "No problem, Officer," he responded, and leaned forward to the glove box to retrieve his registration.

"Freeze!" The sheriff drew his gun and stuck his hand inside the car.

Stunned, Trill slowly eased back into the driver's seat until he felt the tip of the sheriff's revolver at his temple.

"I was going for my registration, man," Trill said slowly. "Don't most people keep their registration in the glove box?"

"You trying to get fresh with me, nigger?" The sheriff cocked his gun.

Trill could feel his blood boiling. Given the opportunity, he would leave the racist redneck stinkin' on the hood of his own police cruiser for his fellow officers to scrape him off.

"You would think that you niggers would know the drill by now, and have these things prepared," the sheriff drawled boldly. "As much shit as y'all stay in, you'd think y'all would pin the damn registration to your collars. Now slowly," Bowman Body said, "open the glove box and retrieve the registration." He paused before adding, "And I said slowly, not like you grabbing for the last piece of chicken out of a bucket of Colonel Sanders."

Trill smelled the scent of trouble like shit from a three-hundred-pound man who just got an enema. He knew Barney Fife was gon' fuck with him until he came up with a reason good enough to stick him. Trill was fully aware that the four thousand grams of crack cocaine in his hiding spot was 3,400 grams more than enough to get him a mandatory life sentence in a federal penitentiary. His intincts told him that he didn't want to trust his life on the chance that this hillbilly didn't impound the truck and stumble up on the stash box. He had to make a move. His next move would be crucial. A convicted felon caught with four kilos of crack cocaine was not a good look. He couldn't take that chance; that was reason enough to give Bowman Body a run for his money. And he intended to do just that.

Trill grabbed the registration from the glove box and turned to hand it to the sheriff. When the sheriff reached inside the truck with his free hand and grabbed hold of the registration, Trill quickly hit the switch to roll the window up while he floored the accelerator at the same time. The powerful Hummer snatched the sheriff off his feet so fast he dropped the pistol, screaming while Trill put the pedal to the metal.

"Who the fuck reaching now? Get yo' hand out the chicken box, cracker!" Trill screamed at Bowman Body. "Get yo' shit out my chicken box, motherfucker!" His adrenaline was pumping, having the upper hand. He knew if he was caught he was gone for life. So he was going out like a real-live gangsta—with a mean fight.

He drove the Humdinger like he was on safari in Africa; the sheriff hung from the side of the car, holding on for dear life, slamming into the door every now and then as the truck dragged him at sixty miles an hour down the road. He went from Barney Fife to Barney Rubble as he ran alongside the automobile.

Bowman Body was swinging from side to side, praying and calling out every scripture in the Bible he'd ever known from his childhood days of going to Vacation Bible School. Once Trill felt like he was deep enough in the sticks and had room and leeway to run and hide, he pushed the window's button down to release the sheriff and slammed on the brakes, throwing the sheriff face first to the ground.

Trill knew that the truck was going to be hot and keeping the beautiful machine would not be an option. This was most likely the only deserted stretch of road he was going to find. He grabbed a piece just in case he had to go to war, pulled off the road and got out of the truck. When Trill opened up the door, Bowman Body was crawling on his belly like a frontline soldier. He was relentless and wasn't going to give up easily. He managed to lunge forward and grab Trill's leg to try to slow him down. Trill laughed at first. He couldn't believe the motherfucker was on his heels. But after he tried to wiggle his leg loose to no avail, he got pissed off.

Trill kicked the sheriff in his face with his new Timbs. Bowman Body's head hit a rock, causing him to bleed like Rick Flair in a cage match. Blood gushed out all over the pavement. Trill didn't waste time. Although his shoes had blood on them, he took off running like a jaguar in the wild. He was mad that he didn't have on the fresh Jordans that he copped earlier from the mall, but Timbs were good in any kind of weather.

It was unlikely that the police would find the drugs, but if they did, it wouldn't matter. Trill's only concern at this point was to get away. He took comfort in knowing that the registered owner of the vehicle didn't know him from a can of paint. He'd paid a friend to pay a friend

$10,000 to put the Hummer in their name. Maybe the best $10,000 he'd ever spent; it pays to think ahead.

It felt like hours as Trill trudged through the trees, mud, rocks and small streams of water. Out of breath and panting, he found a tree to rest against. He knew that he would be there until sundown. Some hunter stopped to help the sheriff, and of course by now backup was on the way, but at least Trill had gotten a fairly decent head start. But no sooner had Trill thought the fading sun was his answer than he heard a sound that put him on the run again. And he needed to move fast. Trill knew he had to shed some weight. As much as he hated to part with it, the first thing to go was his brand-new chinchilla jacket.

The sound of bloodhounds let Trill know that backup and probably some deputized citizens with shotguns were on the scent of his trail. He wasn't too much worried about the bloodhounds; his main concern was them redneck hillbillies who could smell a nigga a mile away. The manhunt was on.

As the pursuit continued, Trill knew that they were closing in on him. Not only was the sound of the hounds getting closer, he could hear the hum of a helicopter entering the area. He couldn't see it yet, but the sound of the whirling blades were distinctive. And just because he couldn't see it didn't mean that it couldn't see him. He knew he was doomed. But he trudged through the woods anyway, hoping no one in the distant houses would see him and give him up. He had no idea where he was going or where he'd end up. The only destination he had in mind was to get the fuck out of redneck county!

As Sunni stood in her kitchen warming up some leftover hot wings from the day before, she went to wash off the sauce that had gotten on her hands. As she looked out of the window over the sink, she could have sworn that she saw something. It was dark, and the light was on in the kitchen, so she could barely see. She flipped the light switch off, allowing her a better view of the rear of her house, and there it was again. It was a person; a black man, and then she zeroed in on the helicopter overhead. When she looked back down from the helicopter, she found herself staring into the eyes of someone in her backyard. She jumped, and a scream slipped out, but then she felt a sense of familiarity. It was the same guy from the Hummer earlier, the one who had given her a visual orgasm at the stoplight.

She knew for a fact that he wasn't volunteering on the manhunt—a black man in this neck of the woods, after sundown? Hell no! Oh, she thought, this brother is definitely being hunted. Sunni knew that if he was caught only one of two things could happen: one, he would be shot dead on the spot, another black man out of the running; or two, he would go straight to jail and the key would be thrown away.

Guydamn, Sunni contemplated. *Why'd he have to end up on* my *doorstep? What am I supposed to do?*

As she watched him looking for a way out, somewhere to run, his face clammy with sweat, her heart went out to him. She quickly ran to the back door, unlocked it and called out, "Come on, come on, I got you!" She waved her arm, motioning him to hurry up.

She shook her head, knowing that she had let her emotions override her intellect for a man once again. Hopefully, this time it won't turn out as bad for her as it did the last time.

Upon seeing the door open, Trill ran inside. He couldn't believe it. He knew that it was only a matter of seconds before they had his black butt hemmed in. This lady being here at the right place, at the right time—he didn't know if it was a setup or what. But for now he was grateful to be able to get some heat and a spot to hide. She slammed the door shut, locking both the security door and the entry door.

He inhaled deeply, trying to catch his breath. "Damn, you saved my ass. Anybody see me?"

Sunni looked out the still open blinds in the kitchen. She separated the blinds just enough to peek out. The coast appeared to be clear. Sunni then closed all the blinds in her house and drew the drapes.

"You can hang out here if you need to," Sunni said flatly when she returned to the kitchen. "You need to use the phone or something?"

"Naw, I just need to lay low and chill for a minute," Trill said and then plopped down on her oversized yellow chaise, exhausted, dehydrated and hungry. Then he thought again. "You got a cell?"

Sunni nodded as she reached for her cell and handed it to him. She listened as he gave someone demands to report his truck stolen. After Trill ended the call, he sat there with a bit of slight anxiety, thinking about the stash box, wondering if the tow company would find it and rip it off. Sunni noticed that his mind was somewhere else, so she tried to redirect his attention.

"Well, I was just about to eat some hot wings," she said casually. "Have some?"

"You got something cold to drink?" he asked. Writing off any negative thoughts about the drugs being gone, he knew he had the best secret hiding place money could buy.

"Sure." She walked over to a cabinet that sat behind the yellow love seat. She opened the refrigerator, introducing a complete stock of liquor, most of which hadn't been uncapped. She then hollered back to Trill.

"I have Coke, Sprite, Corona, Hennessey, Moët, Remy, Grey Goose, orange juice, basically whatever you want," Sunni said, naming the drinks as she scanned the fridge then glanced over to her bar.

"Hennie's good, give me a shot of that on ice." He could feel her eyes burning into him, so he added, "Please."

As she grabbed a glass from the cabinet and poured Trill's drink, she decided that maybe she'd have a drink, too. No use in having dude drinking alone, she thought. After pouring herself a Grey Goose and cranberry, she headed to the kitchen and grabbed some ice from the freezer. When she closed the freezer door and went to turn around, Trill was already standing in the kitchen. He pulled off his sweater and tossed it across the chair beside him as if he lived there. Trill's body caught Sunni off guard. Seeing him in that black wife beater, she could see he'd definitely spent a lot of time working on his body. *Penitentiary body,* she thought as he drank the Henni like it was a shot.

Death Before Dishonor

"You mind?" he asked, referring to the wing he had grabbed off the plate on the table. Then with the same cockiness, he dipped it in the homemade sauce she'd made earlier.

"No, go on," she replied as she watched him take a bite of the wing.

The way he sucked that chicken sent chills up her spine. She watched him put the wing in his mouth and pull off all the meat—with one bite, it was down to the bone.

Okay, she thought. *That mouth could be a useful tool.* "I didn't know being on the run made you that damn hungry," she said as she picked up a wing herself.

Trill looked her over for a couple of seconds. "What's your name?" he asked in between chicken wings. While he waited for her reply, he continued looking her over and focused in on her perky nipples under the T-shirt she was wearing that read, "Don't you wish your girlfriend was hot like me?"

"Sunni," she responded, licking some of the sauce off of her lips.

"When's your birthday?"

"What?" she asked, puzzled.

"Your birthday, when is it?" he repeated.

"September first. Why?"

"Was wondering was you born on a sunny day." He looked around as if he was looking for something specific. Once he spotted the roll of paper towels, he walked over, grabbed one and wiped his hands.

"Actually it was raining."

He nodded as he walked over to her refrigerator, opened it and began rummaging through it to see what was in there.

"Go ahead and make yourself at home," Sunni said sarcastically. She shook her head as if to say, *This shit don't make no sense.*

"Thank you, I think I will." He grabbed a container of fruit punch.

He shook it and, since there seemed to only be enough for one cup, just put the carton up to his mouth and swallowed the last of its contents. He then scanned the kitchen to find the trash can. When he didn't see one, he handed Sunni the empty carton.

"Yo, take care of that for me," he said, followed by a loud belch. She stood, looked at him and rolled her eyes.

"No you didn't," she said—but she put it in the trash.

In a matter of minutes, the humbleness that had come through the door with Trill was gone. He was back in the role of the boss, calling all the shots. Headed back out of the kitchen to give himself a tour of Sunni's house, he had a sudden thought.

"Yo," he said, shaking his head. "I didn't even ask if you had some nigga coming home. I'd hate to have to get buck with a nigga for a little misunderstanding," he stated as he continued his stride, walking through the downstairs of Sunni's house with authority, admiring the bright yellow color scheme she had going on. Sunni was right on his heels like he was a bull in a china shop, making sure he didn't make himself at home with none of her stuff. Trill noticed how everything in her house was somehow connected to the color yellow, which made sense since her name was Sunni.

"Hell no," he said with a snicker. "Ain't no nigga coming here." He turned to look at her. "Well, let me rephrase that, ain't no real nigga livin' like this." He couldn't help but laugh at the thought until another one quickly replaced it. "Seriously though, you expecting any company, any of your girls stopping by?"

Sunni had her arms folded across her chest, "For the most part, my house is off limits. I don't really do much entertaining."

"I like that." Trill nodded with approval.

Sunni rolled her neck. *Like I need this nigga's consent to have company in my daggone house,* she

Nikki Turner

thought. *Who the fuck do this dude think he is anyway?*

"You done came in and took over my house, walk-ing around *my* shit," she said, pointing to her chest, "like you pay bills here and I don't even know your name."

"Trill," he replied firmly and extended his hand. "Nice to meet you, too, and if I ever needed to or wanted to, Miss Lady, I could pay bills here. And since you done brought it up . . ." He went in his pockets and pulled out two stacks of money. "I can pay you for your kind hospitality."

"Naw, you go ahead and keep that. I can hold my owns. Believe that!" she said with an attitude.

"I hear you, ma." Trill put his money away with a grin. "What is it that you do to hold your own?" He looked around at the nice contents of Sunni's home. "You moving weight or something?"

"No, I own my own salon, darling," Sunni said proudly. "Sunny Delight."

"Oh, that's what's up," Trill said as he kicked his Timbs off and sat down on the yellow sofa. "You got a nice place here." He put his feet up on the coffee table and spread his arms on top of the sofa making himself *real* comfortable.

"Look, get yo' guydamn feet off of my table. Nigga, are you crazy?" Sunni snapped. She had had enough of this disrespectful clown and had a mind to throw his ass right back out to the wolves except that it wasn't in her character to hand over a black man to the police.

Not budging a bit, Trill looked up at her and signaled her to come sit down. "Come here. Relax." He patted the spot next to him. "Come sit next to me and tell Big Trill what got you so stressed."

Already, Trill could tell that Sunni had many layers of hostility, but he had enough confidence to try to penetrate through the shield. He was sure there was hope. If there wasn't, she never would have opened up the door for him in the first place. *There's more to her than meets the naked eye*, he mused.

"Nigga, yo' ass was on the fucking run and you come in up in *my* shit taking over like you the damn president and now you want me to come and—"

He cut her off. "I like it when you get aggressive. Finally, some personality. See, most women don't challenge me. They won't stand up to a shot-calling, boss nigga like myself."

"That's because 'most' women don't know any better. They want what you got in your pockets. So, they'll stroke your ego however and do whatever."

"How you know they don't want what's in my pants?" he asked with a cocky demeanor.

She laughed. "That lil' shit?" Boldly, she walked over to him and touched his manhood, which took him by surprise.

"You can't fuck wit' it." He laughed, putting his hand on his dick.

Sunni sucked her teeth and rolled her eyes. "Nigga, get something for me to fuck with." The talk alone was making Sunni hot as a hooker on dollar day. She hadn't had dick in a bunch of months of Sundays. When men were concerned, normally, her guards were up higher than the Great Wall of China.

Sunni had learned to do without the emotional heartaches that came with men; as long as she could get the clit licked she was A-OK with that. Penetration wasn't a biggie for her, especially not with any ol' local nigga. That she saved. She often asked herself, save it for what? But as sexy as Trill's lips and his overall persona were, she felt he wasn't the average Joe Blow. She looked him over as he sat clutching his dick like it was a prized possession. *Nice strong hands . . . hmm, average,* Sunni thought. *Cocky and street with a hint of attractiveness about it . . . cool. A perfectly good dick that fell out of the sky and into my living room . . . PRICELESS!*

"Yo," Trill said, interrupting Sunni's thoughts. "Give me some fresh ice for my drink and hand me that remote."

"You betta get that shit yourself since you seemed to have made yourself at home anyway."

"Cater to me, ma." Trill winked. "I got you, I told you that already. I'ma look out for you real decent before I leave."

"I already told you, I don't need your lil' handouts." Sunni put her hands on her hips.

"Naw, baby, you don't have a choice. I always pays my way," Trill said, shaking his head and holding his hand out for her to give him the remote.

The phone rang, and Sunni was glad. She needed the distraction. Although she should have been putting his tail out of her house, there was something about his confidence and take-charge attitude that did something to her. She was intrigued with him, but to protect her emotions she wanted to get rid of Trill soon. He was starting to make her feel as if she wasn't in control. She was beginning to quiver just a little. This man had no idea how long it had been for her—she didn't have time to play games.

As Sunni sashayed away to get the phone, Trill watched her move across the room toward the cordless phone. The word "Juicy" was printed across the ass of her pants. Sunni wasn't the only one getting hot. This chick had his dick hard like he was still back in the joint. Or maybe it was just a mix of being on the run and now running into her. She'd already told him she didn't have a man coming home, so both his big and little heads were beginning to make plans for the two of them. She looked as juicy and meaty as the chicken wings. Though she was looking rough from a hard day's work, he could see her natural beauty. For some reason the girl from the movie *Belly* popped in his head.

When she got near the phone, she noticed that the receiver wasn't in the base of the charger so she walked into the kitchen real quick and grabbed the phone in the entryway that was mounted to the wall.

"Good evening," Sunni answered.

The voice came through the earpiece loud and clear. It was Ta-Ta.

"Sunni . . . girl, yo' ass left too early!" Ta-Ta shot through the phone, sucking on her tongue ring as she said each word.

"Why? Is everything okay?" Sunni said, turning her back to Trill as she handled her business.

"Yes, but Beatrice had the nerve to show her face in here again after she ain't paid booth rent in two months. Talkin' 'bout she coming to get her shit out yo' office."

"What?" Sunni couldn't believe this shit was happening now. "I'm on my way up there now, Takesha."

"Nawww, girl." Ta-Ta sucked her teeth. "Hell naw! You don't have to come nowhere. Please believe that yo' girl had that shit on lock. Don't no beeyotch come through these doors with the white man."

"The white man?" Sunni raised her voice in astonishment. Trill got up and moved in closer to hear what Sunni was talking about. Sunni took her ear away from the phone, placed her hand over the receiver so that Ta-Ta couldn't hear what she was about to say and then whispered to Trill. "It's just some shop bullshit," she said, easing the look Trill had on his face, "no need to worry."

"Go ahead and handle yo' business," Trill said with a nod. "I like a woman in control of hers."

Trill listened to Sunni converse with Ta-Ta for a few more minutes. He could tell by her tone that she was definitely in control of her business. This was his chance. He'd catch her phat ass off guard.

He started to walk away but then maneuvered himself behind her. Without asking, he moved her hair away from her neck and started kissing the exposed skin. He could feel her tremble.

Feeling the heat rise, Sunni tried to hang up from her call in order to put the fire out.

"Hold on. Wait a minute," Sunni said to Trill, but Ta-Ta thought she was talking to her.

"Finish talking," Trill whispered in her ear softly. "Don't mind me. Get all the beauty shop gossip because this right here going to be the shop talk tomorrow." He took the phone from her, placed her hand on his rock-hard dick and then put the phone back to her ear.

"Hold on, Ta-Ta," Sunni said. She covered the phone with her hand, and in a daring but seductive tone, she said to Trill, "That ain't enough." She probed his shit like she was examining it. "I ain't impressed." She then forwardly stated, "You want to impress me? You want to make my eyes roll back in my head, wait 'til I get off this phone and bring your A-game, head game that is. You did say you wanted to repay me for all my hospitality, right?"

Sunni released her hand from his member like she was throwing that shit back at him before picking up the last chicken wing from the table and licking the top of it like it was a dick, teasing the heck out of him. Mission accomplished.

"Save your chips for the hos who really need your money," she said.

"Yeah, I'm back," she spoke in the phone to Ta-Ta.

Trill stood there speechless, his dick getting harder by the second. If it had been any other ho, she would have found herself lying on the floor recovering from a helli-fied pimp smack. Although it would have been pure disrespect coming from any other broad, for some reason, coming from Sunni, that sassiness made Trill's dick get harder by the second.

"Oh, that bitch had a motherfuckin' locksmith with her, talking about her stuff locked in the office and she hired him to come and unlock the door," Ta-Ta informed Sunni.

"Stop playing!" Sunni replied, taking her eyes off Trill.

"I ain't playing. I pulled her to the side and asked her if I could holla at her for a minute. I took her to the back and . . ."

Ta-Ta was still talking, but those were the last words Sunni heard before she felt Trill's touch. He grabbed her breasts from behind, one in each hand. He squeezed them, pushing them together, and soon felt Sunni responding by her ass wiggling against his groin. She wanted to turn around, but he had her pinned against the wall between the cabinet and the refrigerator. The phone dangled from its cord.

He yanked down her sweats, and spread her knees apart with his leg. She felt her body go weak and could faintly hear Ta-Ta on the phone calling her name.

"Sunni," Ta-Ta yelled. "Sunni, are you still there?"

Hell no, she wasn't there. How could she be with

Trill all up on her? With her pants now down to her ankles and Trill's lips on the cheeks of her ass, she felt him
smearing something on her; when she tilted her head to
get a better look, she found out that it was wing sauce.
Anticipation was killing her, the anticipation of his
tongue entering that sacred spot that hadn't been touched
except by that stupid-ass vibrator since who knows when.

Trill bent her over almost in half and she could feel
the heat of his tongue, combining the tangy sting of the
wing sauce with her own rising temperature. Trill sucked
on her clit the same way he had done those wings earlier,
maybe even harder, that is until she tried to warn him that
she was cumming. But like Swiper the Fox, it was too
late. He had sucked that out of her, too. With Sunni
wasted and limp, Trill turned her around.

"It's your turn now, baby girl," he said as he used his
hands to push down on her shoulders until she found herself on her knees in front of him.

"Unbuckle 'em," he ordered, nodding down toward
his belt. His aggressiveness turned her on.

"Sunnniii, Sunnnniiii!" She was distracted by Ta-Ta's
screams from the phone. She reached to hang up the
phone, then looked at Trill.

"Trill, I don't think you want me to do that," she said,
knowing that if nothing else, in this area she was an

expert and would never lose her touch. That was the one thing that she could thank Scoop for, helping her to master the art of funky cold medina head.

Trill grabbed Sunni by the chin, making her look up at him. She knew she could easily turn this tough guy into a softie by her warm mouth. She unbuckled his pants and his dick popped out of his boxers. It wasn't that it was so thick, but it was so long his last name should have been Longstockings. She'd never be able to deep-throat the entire thing, but she was damn sure gonna try. She started out by slowly licking it, teasing him. After it was wet and slippery, she was ready. She took a deep breath and began swallowing, a little at a time until she got her rhythm. She worked it until he began to pulsate and his knees began to buckle.

"Damn girl," Trill moaned. "You got it all."

She could taste little bits of his cum and she heard him faintly moaning, but she wouldn't let him cum in her mouth. She slowly pulled back, letting his dick slide back out across her tongue. With him out of breath, she felt like she had seen and conquered. She whispered, "Who's that beeyotch, nigga?"

"Baby, you are! You are! No doubt about it."

Sunni knew he was about to explode, but no way did she want him to waste a good nut on the kitchen floor.

She stood up and led him into her bedroom, where it was a guarantee that she was gon' make that nigga see the sunshine, even in the middle of the night. Giving a new definition to her given name.

You Can Take
The Girl Out Of
The City,

But You Can't Take The City Out Of The Girl!

$\mathcal{A}$fter a long night of making love, Sunni was beside herself. She hadn't been fucked that good since . . . Hell, she had never been screwed that good. But even so, it was still categorized in her mind as a one-night stand. She had to get rid of him. Sunni turned over and looked at the clock before looking over at that fine specimen laying up in her bed. Like the true down ass chick she knew she was, she also knew that it was time for that man to break out.

Sunni got up, showered and got herself together. She wasn't the least bit quiet, hoping that all the ruckus she was making would wake Trill so that she wouldn't have to. Evidently being on the run and all that screwing must have put him in a deep sleep because he didn't budge.

"Rise and shine," Sunni shouted, snatching the covers off of Trill. *Hmm,* Sunni thought after witnessing his bare tight-muscled ass laid across her bed. *Maybe I ought to reconsider my plans for the day.* But then she remembered her motto, Money Over Niggas, and the thought left her mind just as quickly as it had come. "Get *up!*" she stressed.

As Trill felt the covers being pulled off of him, he rolled over and wiped his eyes. He looked at the clock: 6:07 A.M. They had just gone to sleep a little over three hours ago.

"Come on, yo. Get back in the bed," Trill said to her, noticing that she was fully dressed. She was wearing a cute J.Lo velour sweat suit and had her hair down. Her lips looked edible, smothered in a clear gloss.

Seeing that she was fully dressed let Trill know that she had been up for a while and that he had slept comfortably around her while she did whatever she needed to do to get ready. Resting and sleeping were things Trill didn't do around just anyone. He could count on one hand the amount of people he trusted well enough to sleep around, and have a finger or two left. Slipping, sleeping, they were one and the same. Getting caught doing either by the wrong person could cost him his life.

"I can't sleep. I gotta go get my money," Sunni answered matter-of-factly.

He pulled the covers back over his body. "Man, I got you for the day. Come lay up with Daddy."

"Some of us gotta work. I don't have the luxury of laying up while a nigga take care of me and I damn sho' ain't going to let no nigga lay in my shit while I'm slaving all day."

"You don't have to slave."

"I do have to work like a slave so I can eat like a master."

He smiled, loving the hustle in the woman standing before him. That was something Precious, his girlfriend, who seemed to have slipped his mind while he was slippin' his dick in Sunni, didn't have. Precious wasn't getting up at the crack of dawn to go to work. The only thing she would wake up that early for was the early bird sale at Saks.

Sunni pulled the covers off of Trill for the second time and stood over him with her hands on her hips. "Look, you need to get up. There's a towel, washcloth and a new toothbrush in the bathroom on the counter."

Trill gave her a long stare before getting up. He walked over to the master bathroom that was connected to the bedroom and took a piss. While using the commode he looked around the bathroom. There were suns and sunshine rays all around him, even down to the toilet seat.

"Sunni, what the fuck you got all these suns in here for?" he asked, referring to the bathroom décor.

"So yo' butt can have a great day, motherfucker. That's what fo'. Now hurry up and take one of those minuteman showers 'cause I got somewhere to be."

Trill turned on the water in the shower and then called out to Sunni, "What you know about a minuteman shower?"

"Don't be fooled by my good looks," Sunni warned. "The judge wasn't affected at all by my cute and innocent face. He made me press that bunk and do that time."

Trill chuckled and got in the shower. He walked back into the bedroom with a towel wrapped around his waist, dripping wet from the hot shower.

"Where you need to be dropped off at?" Sunni asked him. She handed him his wife beater and sweater. "Get ready. I'm in a hurry."

"I need to go to Chesterfield then to Churchill," he replied as he got dressed.

"I ain't no van-to-go service," Sunni snapped.

"Look, I ain't strapped," he started to explain to her,

using his hands. "When I was running, I had to throw my gun away and I can't hit the streets without my burner. It's just that simple. Now I'ma need you to run me to Chesterfield to get me one and then drop me off in Churchill."

"That's all you stressing about? A burner?"

"What you mean is that all I'm stressing about? I'm from the jungle and you know what happens to the weak animals in the jungle." He paused, waiting for her to respond. When she didn't he continued, "They become part of the food chain."

"Just like I had you last night, I got you again. I'ma let you borrow mine." Sunni went over to her purse and pulled out a .40-caliber Ruger.

"What da fuccckkk?" Trill exclaimed. He couldn't believe this little woman was carrying such a big gun.

She held up the gun and handed it to him. "I never loan my shits out. My gun is like my insurance card. I don't never leave home without it."

"Why you packing, ma?" he asked, taking the gun from her.

"I live alone and work late at night. And I shouldn't have to tell you that there's all types of lunatics running around. And while you bullshitting," she said with a pause, "you could be one."

"Me, a lunatic?" He laughed and shook his head. "Those white boys Ted Bundy, Jeffrey Dahmer, now they were lunatics." He put the piece of steel in the back of his pants and proceeded to put on his shoes so they could head out.

5

Down for the Cause

The city was fienin' for a huge event, and the town's internationally bestselling author, Nikki Turner, blessed the city of Richmond with a series of activities celebrating the launch of her latest masterpiece, *Forever a Hustler's Wife*. She wanted to raise money for the G-Unity charity, so she played off the theme of her street life books and decided to have a "diamonds and furs" party to raise money to help increase literacy and advertise her new book at the same time. It was promoted as a Baller's Ball, challenging rappers, ballplayers, shot callers, bosses and all the Robin Hoods of the hoods to show up, floss and ball out of control for a good cause. The author made sure there were a limited amount of tickets available, which created an even bigger buzz for the event. People always wanted what they couldn't have.

The crowd came in sellout numbers. Lloyd Banks from G-Unit was one of the MCs. Olivia from G-Unit hosted along with radio personalities Mahogany Brown and Wendy Williams. They each claimed a spot on the red carpet and interviewed the celebrity guests as they arrived. Although many limelight celebrities came out and showed love and unity for the author and her cause, her hometown big hats, fans and ghetto celebrities didn't disappoint.

Trill and his boys did it up real big in the gear department for Ms. Turner. Trill was wearing a simple, well-tailored black suit that complemented his sexy frame. While his suit may have been simple, there was nothing ordinary about the full-length chinchilla that he sported. The coat made the one he shed while running from the police look like child's play. He was carrying a black marble cane with his name embedded in diamonds down the side.

His crew held it down as well. None of them came half-ass. Trill's cousin Noc-Noc, who had come from Detroit about a year ago when Trill needed a thoroughbred player on his team, was used to sporting different animal skins to keep warm. So getting dressed for this event came natural to him: He wore a three-piece chocolate-brown suit with the mink jacket and hat to match. Though Trill and Mont had been down since the sandbox, blood was always thicker than mud any day. Noc-Noc believed that family was all he had, and his mother and three little sisters were what he went all out for by any means necessary. He knew if he didn't get paid, they didn't eat, so him being in Richmond for his cousin was a lot of hard work and hardly any play.

Mont believed that his light, reddish complexion, curly hair and hazel eyes were God's gift to women. So he decided to keep it basic; he sported a black leather suit with a full-length Alan Fur to match.

Trill's other boy, Seven, had on a tight-fitting shirt to show off his penitentiary build. It made the females approach him and ask if he was a personal trainer. He carried his fur in his hand. His iced-out necklace complimented by Austrian crystal frames had plenty eyes on him. They all were playing their position. Not only were they out flossing, wanting to be seen, but in their camp, it was always work first and play later. Trill's first priority for his crew was to case the place to find out what potential victims were worth their time. That was why the only person in the crew in costume working was Jon-Jon.

Jon-Jon had been Trill's cellmate for three of the five-year stretch Trill had done. He was clean-cut, brown-skinned and slim, standing six feet tall and sporting a bow tie. Jon-Jon wasn't a killer, but he was a genius when it came to computers, security codes and any other technical task that required computer savvy. He hated blood, but he loved money, and that was what he and Trill had in common.

A few days before Trill was released from jail, Jon-Jon made a pact with him.

"Look, Trill, this is the deal," Jon-Jon said from the top bunk as he stared at the ceiling. "I ain't coming back here, but I don't want to be broke, either."

"No shit," Trill agreed from the bottom bunk.

"You got the heart to kill for what you want and the know-how to execute the plan. I got the heart to rape a computer and the brains to get away with it before anyone ever figures out that sucker is bleeding from all the info I've stolen."

"What you trying to say?"

"Well," Jon-Jon said and jumped down from his bunk, "if you do what you do best and I do what I do best, together our potential is damn near unstoppable."

Jon-Jon extended his hand to Trill. They shook, and they'd been working together ever since.

On this particular evening, Jon-Jon was posing as a photographer from an overseas magazine that had a catchy name, but no one had really heard of it. Nonetheless, they were much obliged to have him there for some international press. Jon-Jon was slick with his game. Bruce Willis in *The Jackal* didn't have shit on him

As soon as Trill and his crew stepped off the red carpet, they were greeted by a fine Asian chick, gracefully extending a sterling silver tray with champagne-filled glasses surrounding a bottle of Dom. They each helped themselves to a glass, Noc-Noc helping himself to the entire bottle. Trill then placed two bills on the tray and shooed the girl off.

Trill looked around for Sunni as he mingled a bit and then made his way into the party to their reserved booth.

Soon after Trill arrived, the only person who did it bigger on the red carpet than Trill and his crew showed up on the red carpet. Diego arrived in a four-door Maserati, sporting a flamboyant sky-blue suit that was the same color as the foreign car. And just to be certain that he wasn't half doing it, but whole thangin' it, on his pinky he wore an eight-carat, custom-made blue diamond ring. He sported a pair of exotic-looking petite twins whom he'd flown in from Miami just for this event. They were holding on to his arms like he was a clutch bag, and both beautiful women wore blue contacts to match their blue diamond necklaces. Diego had another girl close on his heels who was wearing a blue fox jacket and pulling a Louis Vuitton roller suitcase.

"What's in the roller?" Mahogany Brown asked Diego.

"It's for da kids," he said in his Cuban accent. "We're here to support d'kids. It's a charity and we intend to spend lotta money for d'kids."

Diego was born to a black father and a Cuban mother. His ties to the Cuban Mafia were bound by his mother's blood. He possessed no love for nothing, besides his own bloodline. By the time he was sixteen, he had his hands all over South Florida's drug trade, and by the time he was twenty years old, he had three more states under his belt. Hearing the rumors of all the money that there was to be made in Virginia, Diego put his foot in the door and had a great thing going on. It was something about Richmond that made him get the urge to not only work hard, but to play hard as well—not all the time, but he would on occasion let his hair down, unbutton his collar and just shit on niggas, and this just happened to be one of those times. This was an event that he definitely pulled out all his toys for and amused not only the town and his workers, but himself, too.

As Diego entered the party, Trill studied everyone that Diego gave dap to and watched closely who ordered how many bottles. Trill's comrades knew what had Trill's attention.

"Look at dat nigga," Seven said as they observed Diego making his way down the red carpet. "Best believe that's a mark that we can probably retire off."

"Sheeit, man, the streets are talking and if you believe what the streets say, that nigga is supplying over sixty percent of the city and got his hands in three different states."

"All money ain't good money," Mont said and looked at Seven then at Trill.

"Man, if I ain't learned nothing from watching *The Godfather*, a million times I learned one thing, and that's anybody can be hit," Noc-Noc interjected.

Trill digested the comments from each of his comrades and drained the last of his drink before he spoke.

"There's a time and a place for everything." Trill smiled.

Diego spent quite a great deal of time with one particular set of guys. It didn't take Trill long to figure out that some were local and the others were out-of-towners. Trill continued to observe them until he saw a local chick approach one of the fellas. In a moment a lover's quarrel erupted. Trill silently stood by and watched as the girl got madder and madder. That's when he tapped Mont on the shoulder and motioned to him to keep his eyes and ears on the situation as it unfolded.

Mont inconspicuously cruised until he was within earshot and could hear everything that was going down between the couple.

"Lee, I'm sick of this shit!" the girl yelled, her long black ponytail swinging from left to right with every snap of her neck. "I was the first person you met when you came down here and I've held you down ever since. All yo' shit is in my fucking name. I sacrificed e'rything for you, and every time I turn around, some no-good bitch is in your face."

"Damn, Tiffany. Don't come up in here and start with that same ole shit," Lee said, putting his hand up in ol' girl's face as if she wasn't shit. "Save it," he said, and then took a sip of his drink, pointing out his pinky finger as if he was sipping tea.

"Muthafucka." Tiffany pushed his hand from in front of her face. "This is how you gon' try to play me in front of them bitches? You gon' spare their feelings when I'm the one that's always there for you? You know these washed-out hos don't mean you no good."

"And you do? You mean me some good by nagging the fuck out of me?" He dug down in his pocket and

DEATH BEFORE DISHONOR

pulled out a two-inch stack of money. He handed her a couple of hundred-dollar bills and then looked over her

shoulder. "Take this. Who you here with? Go buy you and your girls something to drink, something to put in your goddamn mouth, that way you won't have to come up over here runnin' it."

"Leeee!" she cried out in shock, unable to believe he was actually talking to her like she was a nobody. "What's this about? Your boys?" She looked around, knowing that Lee was trying to front off the embarrassment of his girl getting in his ass around his boys.

"Go 'head now," he said, giving her another bill. "And that's it. Take that, and bounce. I ain't trying to have no bitch on my back constantly bothering me about another bitch." He pushed Tiffany out of the way. "See ya when I see ya." He then walked away.

Tiffany stood there looking like she was ready to cry. She tried hard to conceal the tears in her eyes but she couldn't keep them from filling up. Trill could see the hurt and the pain, and his gut told him she was ripe to be exploited

He motioned with his head for Mont. Mont then made his way back over to Trill.

"Yo, what's up?" Mont asked Trill.

"Go ahead and handle your business," Trill said to

Mont as he nodded toward Tiffany. Just then he noticed someone he recognized heading across the room.

"I got her," Mont said, looking at Trill with a cocky expression.

"Make moves then," Trill said as he took a final sip from the glass of champagne he was holding and made his way through the crowd to the room where the book signing was going on, the same room where the familiar face faded off to.

Sunni cut the line to get her book signed. She was looking good in her mink miniskirt and a matching fitted mink jacket. Trill couldn't recall all that cleavage she was flashin'. The wonders a Wonder Bra could work.

"Yo, what's up, Sunshine?" Trill asked, creepin' up from behind.

She didn't recognize the voice, but when she turned around, she saw a pair of eyes she'd never forget. "This long line that hasn't moved in the past ten minutes, that's all," she tried to sound nonchalant.

"You ain't been standing in it." He smiled. "I just saw you cut the line."

"That's because I had to sit down. They ran out of books because some Cuban motherfucker gon' pay for like ten cases of books so that he could donate them to the charity. He went so far as to get some goons to take the books now like he gon' donate them tonight. We've been waiting for them to bring some more books in."

"You bullshitting?"

Trill had completely ignored Cher, Sunni's best friend, who was standing in line with her, until she added her two cents. "That nigga, Diego, is really getting money," Cher said. "I don't know what that nigga's story is. That motherfucker rolled up in here in a blue Maserati with three bitches and done bought up everything."

"Don't get any ideas, Cher," Sunni warned her friend. "He's either the Feds or the Feds is on his trail. In this town with a blue Maserati, you can best believe it's one or the other."

Trill laughed at the irony. "Sunni and Cher? That's funny! You kidding me, right?"

"Nope, that's exactly how we became best friends. The white Sonny and Cher was together for years so we decided so would we," Sunni said defensively.

"So, what about Trill and Sunni?" Trill asked.

"What about it?" She threw the question back at him.

Trill cut to the chase. "When can I see you again?"

"With all due respect, we fulfilled each other's needs." She looked into his eyes. "No further obligations are needed. And before I forget, I'm going to need you to return my merchandise to me at your earliest convenience."

For a few seconds, Trill was at a loss for words. Rejection wasn't something that he was used to.

"So, it's like that?" he replied.

Without hesitation she assured him, "Straight like that." She answered without a second thought.

"I'm peace wit that right now." And he walked away like he'd just won a prize.

He turned and peeped in the other room. Leaving his embarrassment in the book-signing room, he focused in on Mont giving Tiffany a hug, and he knew that Mont had the info they needed.

A scorned heart always needs an ear to listen, Trill thought, displaying a smile as he walked away from Sunni. His work was damn near finished; he just had to make his charitable donations and arrange to get some books and then head to the lab to conjure up his next get-rich-quick scheme.

6

Cold
Cash

On the outskirts of Richmond, inside the house in Caroline County, four guys and two broads were entertaining themselves. Lee, one of Diego's lieutenants, was in the bedroom laying pipe to some hoochie momma he had picked up at the club. Lee's worker, Redd, and a big-chested chick were watching a movie in the living room, and two other guys, Mannie and Moe, were laid back playing *50 Cent: Bulletproof* on PlayStation in another bedroom. All of a sudden a base-ball came flying through the living room window. The loud noise startled everyone in the entire house. Lee was trying to pull his pants up while running to the front of the house to see what was going on. Redd stopped what he was doing and ran to the bedroom window. Mannie and

Moe dropped the game and ran to the front of the house. Redd looked out but didn't see anything. Baffled, he headed to the living room to scope out the situation. Redd started to raise hell once he realized that it was just a baseball through the window causing all that commotion. The neighborhood kids always managed to annoy him.

"These motherfuckin' kids," Redd spat. "I'm going out here and beat they asses myself. Motherfuckers wanna keep kickin' that 'It Takes a Village,' well, here it goes." Redd headed toward the room Mannie and his boy had been chilling in. "These badass motherfuckers shouldn't be out this time of night anyway. You'd think they'd be in the house sleepin' on a fucking school night," he mumbled as he slipped his shoes on so he could go outside and address the kids.

Before he could even open the front door, another baseball came through the window. Then the next sound was a loud crash, but this time the noise came from the back of the house. The noise startled everyone and demanded their attention. It even sent the hoochie momma out from the back bedroom to the front of the house. Moe, the other dude playing the video game, reached for his gun. Before anyone realized that the baseballs were only a ploy to get everyone to the front of the house, the back door was on the floor and Trill and his crew, dressed in black and wearing ski masks, raided the house like the Feds.

Moe raised his .357, but he wasn't fast enough. Before Moe could squeeze off a round, two bullets from Trill's MP-5 had entered the front of his head, creating a portrait of blood and brain matter onto the walls behind him. Mannie stood there in shock until Trill turned the gun toward him. Then he just lay down on the floor without saying a word. Before the hoochie momma could get down the hall good, Mont hit her with a left hook, sending her straight on her back. Once she hit the ground, she moaned and looked up at him.

"Bitch, facedown if you don't wanna die!" he warned her.

"Lay down, motherfuckers!" Noc-Noc yelled.

Trill and Noc-Noc held everyone in the room at gunpoint while Mont and Jon-Jon began searching the house to find what they came for. Seven handcuffed the big-chested chick and both Mannie and Redd, leaving Lee the last man standing.

"Nigga, you going to tell us where the money and work at?" The question from Trill was more of a matter of fact.

Lee stared Trill down.

"Lee, please, tell 'em what they need to know," the big-chested chick begged him with tears running down her cheeks. "Shit. I wish I knew, I would tell. These niggas ain't playing," she added in between sobs.

"That's why you don't know, bitch," Redd said quickly. "Don't say nothin' to 'em, man."

"Listen to your bitch, man," Trill suggested to Lee in a dry, diplomatic tone. "Give us what we came for."

Once Seven had finished cuffing everybody, he patted them down, taking their wallets, IDs, jewelry, pocket cash and anything else of any value and placed everything into a bag.

"Man, you gon' tell me willingly or you gon' make me kill e'rybody in this mufuckin' house, bitches *and* niggas," Noc-Noc said as he looked at Lee through the slits of the black knit ski-mask he wore. Lee hesitated for just a split second, but when Noc-Noc never broke his stare, Lee recognized the hunger for murder in his eyes.

"Lee, this shit is real," the half-naked girl cried out. "It's real, Lee."

Lee took a deep breath. "Man." Pausing, he mumbled behind his teeth and under his breath, "Man, it's in the deep freezer."

"What? Speak up, I can't hear you!" Noc-Noc ordered.

Lee cleared his throat and spoke clearly, trying not to antagonize the situation any more than it already was.

DEATH BEFORE DISHONOR

"The deep freezer. It's in the deep freezer under the rack where the boxes of steaks are."

"Yo," Trill called out to Jon-Jon and Mont. "In the deep freezer. Check it."

Seven stood in front of the guys and looked through the wallets. Once he got to Lee's he took a picture of his daughter out. He turned it over and read the back out loud. "Deja Monet, huh? She sure is real cute. Pretty lil' thing." He then held the picture up.

"How old is she?" Trill asked.

Seven continued to read the back of the photo. "Seven years old."

"She's older than two so she can be dealt with if need be," Noc-Noc said.

Lee knew he was between a rock and a hard place and that these dudes caught him shitting with his pants down. They had his address and his daughter's photo.

"The yeo is in the steak boxes, man," Lee said as he thought about his little girl. "The combination to the safe is 23 to the left three times, 12 to the right two times and hit on 17."

"We got it," Mont yelled back moments later.

"You a good father, man," Noc-Noc said as he patted Lee on the back.

Jon-Jon opened the small fire safe and came face-to-face with more than nine hundred thousand dollars in cash. "Now that's some cold cash right there," he exclaimed with a smile.

Jon-Jon and Trill loaded the safe and steak boxes into the van. Six of the surplus steak boxes held more than ten kilos of raw cocaine.

"That's everything," Noc-Noc said as he came back in from loading the van.

They started to exit the house when Noc-Noc turned to Redd and said, "Before you go giving somebody else bad advice, next time I bet you'll think twice." He then sent three bullets to Redd's chest, just to get his point across. See, Noc-Noc was wild like that—young, out of control and certainly trigger-happy. "I guess it won't be a next time, huh?"

Then he turned to the others and pointed his gun at them, and Big Chest just started screaming at the top of her lungs. Noc-Noc laughed.

Lee and Mannie went to see Diego to tell him what happened, and that they didn't have any clue who was behind the black masks. A message they both dreaded giving him.

DEATH BEFORE DISHONOR

"What the fuck you mean you don't know what happened to my fucking money and product?" Diego screamed.

"It was like them niggas had the inside scoop. They had us all mapped out and shit," Lee informed Diego.

"They were professionals," Mannie added. "Shit, we were sitting ducks."

"You come here and you tell me ten keys of my uncut product gone, and you say to me you have no inkling who's responsible." He threw up his hands. "Nine hundred thousand dollars of my money is poof, gone!" He raised his voice. "And two of my workers is dead! All you can tell me is it was professionals and you were sitting ducks. Is that right?" he asked Mannie while Lee remained silent.

"Yes, it won't shit we could do," Mannie spoke back in frustration.

Diego paced the floor looking at his disobedient workers. After about five steps, he pulled his gun from his holster and shot Mannie in the chest. Lee's first instinct was to see about his comrade, but he knew better unless he wanted to be lying next to him. He stood there trying not to perspire, and like a trained puppy, he waited for his master to give him instructions.

"Shit like this can't happen again," Diego said through his clenched teeth. "Put your ears to the streets, find out who is behind this."

Lee nodded and knew he, too, was skating on thin ice.

7

The
Good Life

rill walked up to the freshly refinished pecan French doors of his and Precious' seven-bedroom suburban home. He had to admit, the shit was hot. Ripped straight from the pages of *Better Homes and Gardens*. Trill had his girlfriend, Precious, to thank for this extravagant home, that and his long hours in the street perfecting his craft.

Moments after Trill placed the key into the door allowing his Air Force Ones to hit the gray, black and pearl-colored marble floor, Precious surfaced wearing the latest Prada ensemble, with her mouth twisted up with complaints. It was amazing to Trill that even in the midst of all their beautiful things—the waterfall in the study to the right of the doorway, the crystal chandelier in the foyer, the imported cream Napa leather chaise in the corner, and the 18-karat-gold mantelpiece over the fireplace in the living room—Precious, in all of her splendor, could manage to make even the most beautiful things in the world seem so unappealing sometimes.

"It's about time you finally came home," Precious said, rolling her eyes and then placing her hands on her hips, displaying her already inflamed attitude. He didn't need a match to get her started because, as usual, she was already on fire.

"Didn't you see us calling you? Lil' Stanley wanted to speak to his dad."

Trill managed to tune her out, something he had mastered over time, as he slid out of his shoes to avoid yet another opportunity to get yelled at for walking on the floor in them.

"When I called here earlier today, you never said anything about Lil' Trill wanting to speak to me." Although he had become accustomed to her bitching and complaining, he knew deep down that that was just part of her way of expressing her love for him. He knew her little games were her means of having some control over their situation.

Precious had been Trill's girlfriend for a little more than six years. She was everything any man could want and more. Her long, thin frame, drop-dead gorgeous features and her aspiration to become a high-fashion runway model were her claim to fame. With a peanut butter–like complexion, long jet-black hair and her straight diva attitude, she would have definitely secured a spot in the fashion industry—if it weren't for her missing leg. Even so, she could've been with almost any man she wanted. But for some reason her heart desired Trill as his heart desired her and had from the first moment they laid eyes on each other.

In the beginning of their relationship, Trill was solely attracted to Precious because of her looks. Precious was a silver dollar, fuck, a dime piece. He felt that with a girl like Precious on his arm, he couldn't go wrong. She walked the walk and talked the talk in terms of a woman's worth. And for that, he valued her. Precious played her position to a T, and Trill knew it. When the stakes were high, she rode with him. And even when times got tough, she rode for him. After many years of her "reppin the cause," Trill knew that Precious could definitely hold the title of "the one," and with that title, he vowed to be loyal and stay by her side.

He watched her as she stood in front of him, her body a little disproportioned due to her injury, but her presence still strong.

"Damn, can't I ever come home to peace?" Trill said. "Why you gotta start with the mouth the minute a nigga come through the door?"

"You see this shit?" Precious said as she rolled up her pant leg to reveal the constant reminder of her loyalty to him. "This enables me to talk shit when you come through the door. Especially when I've been blowing you up all night and you haven't responded."

Trill looked at her leg and knew her point, again, had been made. Although it was the finest prosthetic leg money could buy, it was still a constant reminder of her commitment to him. And because of that, he allowed her to indulge on any occasion she saw fit.

Precious had gotten caught in the cross fire of a robbery gone bad. It was a plot against Trill, which ultimately resulted in him doing five years in the penitentiary and Precious losing one of her legs. When he went to prison, Precious stepped up to the plate in many ways. She took custody of Trill's only son by another woman, while nursing herself through rehabilitation and having to learn to walk again. Not a day went by that she didn't hold it down for them while he was away. She accepted every collect call he'd ever made; visited him every weekend; fed, cleaned and clothed his child; and through the power of her own street savvy, maintained a home for both Lil' Trill and herself. It wasn't the *Better Homes and Gardens* mansion where they lived now, but it was a roof over their heads.

For that he owed her big-time, and not only did he give her the world and everything in it; he gave her his loyalty. If it wasn't for him getting caught slipping, she might still have her leg. If only he could go back to that one night. They were out having a good time when two thirsty cats with an itch tried to rob him. The guys didn't bank on him bucking on their guns, which turned a robbery into a calamity, costing Precious her right leg and modeling career. It was her dedication to him and his son that kept her in his personal space forever. And because he was the type of man who gave his word and stuck to it, he knew that no matter how tight or messed up things got between the two of them, he was there for life.

"Trill, I be so worried about you when you don't answer your phone," Precious cooed.

"I was working," he huffed, kissing her dryly on the cheek.

He dropped his keys in the crystal glass bowl on the counter and went into Lil' Trill's room to play Xbox with his son. He knew it was only a matter of time before Precious would come in and interrupt. She was the jealous type and he and Lil' Trill were having way too much fun without her.

"How you know how to play this good?" Trill asked his son.

"Uncle Mont showed me," Lil' Trill answered, not taking his eyes off the game.

The power to the 36" plasma screen went off as Precious stood at the doorway holding the remote insisting that Lil' Trill heed his bedtime.

"Aw, Mom," he whined.

"Aw Mom, nothing," Precious teased. "You know it's already an hour past your bedtime, lights out."

"But, Mom, I was just about to beat Dad." He sighed as he threw the controller down on the floor.

"I don't care. Your father knew better than to come in here trying to play with you this late anyway." Her eyes cut to Trill. "He's just trying to avoid our grown folk conversation, but I got something for him, too. Now off to bed, and don't have me say it again."

Lil' Trill climbed into his twin-sized sleigh bed while Trill tucked him in. His kiss good night was long and drawn out. He smiled as he patted his son's head and whispered, "Does she look like she's getting mad?"

Lil' Trill peeped over Trill's shoulder and nodded.

With his front teeth missing and a big smile, he whispered back, "Yeah, Daddy. She's real pissed off."

Trill laughed and then rose from his son's side. "I'll see you in the morning, lil' man."

When he walked out of the room, he could tell that she was still upset with him, which only made him chuckle. She followed him as he walked into the kitchen to grab a beer from the Sub-Zero refrigerator. Trill loved that Precious made sure they had only the latest appliances and furnishings in their house. From the plasma-screen televisions to the state-of-the-art kitchen appliances to the built-in indoor barbecue grill. Yeah, the house was off the chain.

Precious stood near the wall-length aquarium with her eyes fixed on Trill. She pouted as he continued to subtly ignore her.

"I know you just put him back in bed because you want some attention from Daddy, huh?" Trill said, cracking open the can of beer and slurping up the suds that seeped through the top opening.

"You know it," Precious said, walking toward him. "But I want you to promise to answer the phone when I call."

"You still on that?" Trill pressed his body against hers.

"It's just so frustrating when I call you and you don't answer."

"Sometimes, out there, I can't answer the phone. How you think I feel?"

"Well, baby, I'm sorry it's just . . ." She lowered her head, hoping that he would believe her sincerity at his sympathy.

He moved away from her and walked toward the bathroom.

"You gotta trust me," he shouted back as he reached for the knob on the glass sink bowl and ran some water over his face. He then made his way to the shower where he turned on the water, allowing the dual showerheads to spray out full throttle.

"Trill, you seem to forget that while you're out there in those streets, I'm here holding us down at home. If you would just act like I matter half the time, I wouldn't have to nag you."

He didn't respond, instead he pulled off the rest of his clothes, exposing his muscular frame. He knew if anything could shut Precious up momentarily, it was the possibility of them having sex. He walked into the shower, leaving the doors slightly ajar. As the warm water trickled down his body, he looked over at her.

"Now what did you want to talk about?" he asked.

She smiled and was quiet for a minute. She didn't know whether she wanted to fuck the shit out of her man now or tell him about the money she needed to go shopping.

"Boo," she started, "Neiman's sent me this thirty percent off coupon and I want to go to the sale tomorrow to get some things. I'm going to go to the one at Tysons Corner, and while I'm up there I want to go in Gucci and look at their new spring arrivals." Trill didn't respond. "My sales rep called me about some things that came in today and she has them on hold for me." Just to sweeten the cake she threw in, "She's holding some nice men's things, too."

"What you gon' need this time?" He sighed.

"Like, ummm, ten, no, make it fifteen. That's all."

"I thought you said you wanted to save to get your modeling agency off the ground. Blowing fifteen Gs on clothes ain't gon' get you that modeling agency."

"I do want to save and I am. I'm saving thirty percent off the regular price."

"No kidding."

Trill exited the shower and wrapped himself with the towel that Precious had waiting for him. He gave her that "Okay, come fuck me now" look and she moved in close and took her cue as if she could read his mind. She kneeled down and showed her man some love. When he came in her mouth, she gargled that cum around in her mouth like it was some minty mouthwash, before finally swallowing it. He knew that although he thought he was calling the shots, he'd just been played.

"Look, babe," Trill said. "I'ma have to do something right quick. When I get back I'm gonna finish this off."

She smiled, satisfied with her victory. "I'll be waiting for you, Daddy."

Trill looked back at Precious and knew that he definitely wanted to finish what he started. He had to count the money from the robbery first, so even though he wanted Precious more than ever, he knew that in this case he had to handle business before he could enjoy the fruits.

He sat down at the kitchen table and counted all the blood money. He then pulled out a piece of paper and wrote down the cuts once he decided who'd get what. He wanted to make sure everything was kosher for tomorrow's meeting with the crew. Once all his accounting was done, he headed to the bedroom.

But once he had finished his bedroom business, he found that every time he closed his eyes he wished he was in bed with Sunni instead of Precious. Although Precious was far prettier than Sunni and the sex was way more explicit between him and Precious, there was something about the chemistry between him and Sunni that was so intense. The fact that Sunni was so independent also attracted him.

He looked over at the clock; it read 6:59 A.M. He pulled the covers back and hopped in the shower to wash away the sticky and sweaty result of the off-the-chain sex he and Precious had experienced throughout the night. Once he got out of the shower, he went over to his oversized walk-in closet to get dressed. He heard Precious getting Lil' Trill ready for school. Before he knew it, she was standing at the closet door.

"My, my, my," Precious said in a singsong voice. "You are up early."

He didn't speak for a minute, his eyes scanning the closet for something to wear. "Good morning to you, too, baby," he finally said.

"You going somewhere?"

He nodded. "As a matter of fact, I am on my way out. I'll drop Lil' Trill off at school since, let you tell it, I don't spend enough quality time with him anyway. Plus, I thought you got a sale to go to?"

Trill got dressed and went into Lil' Trill's room and said, "Saddle up, lil' man. It's time to roll."

"Okay, Daddy," Lil' Trill said, grabbing his backpack

from the back of the chair to his desk. "I'm ready." Trill led him by the hand and headed downstairs where Precious was waiting in the kitchen.

When Trill looked over at the bag on the kitchen table, he noticed that it wasn't folded the way he had left it. He knew there was no need to check—he knew that Precious had been inside.

After dropping Lil' Trill off at school, he dropped off the money at the stash house, an apartment located in the Shockoe Bottom district of Richmond. He remembered to snatch up Sunni's gun, a perfect and legitimate excuse to make his way down her path. He knocked out a couple of things he needed to do first before arriving at Sunny Delight.

Gangsta
Mathematics

Trill arrived at Sunny Delight Beauty Salon and was greeted by the on-duty receptionist.

"Do you have an appointment, sir?" the receptionist asked.

"Naw, but let Sunni know that Trill is out here for her," he said in his usual cocky demeanor.

The receptionist picked up the phone and called to the back to let Sunni know that she had a guest.

"Ummm, can you let Sunni know that a gentleman by the name of Trill who doesn't have an appointment is demanding to see her," the receptionist exaggerated to Sunni's shampoo girl, who had answered the phone. Then she said, "Okay, I'll let him know."

She hung up the phone and turned her attention to Trill. "Her assistant said that she is swamped and won't be able to come out here," she said. Then the receptionist moved her attention back to the tabloid magazine she was reading before Trill had entered the salon, leaving him standing there.

He decided to sit down. He figured he would just have to wait her out. Twenty minutes went by while Trill paged through the magazines and saw a few chicks he knew come in and out; now the phones were ringing off the hook. He was amazed at how the shop's receptionist held it under control. Once there was a pause in the phone ringing, he approached the receptionist.

"Look, miss, what's your name?" Trill asked.

"Sissy," she replied.

He leaned in to speak to her. "Look, I've been waiting patiently for Sunni to come out here. I don't have much time and I need you to do me a favor," he said as he plucked off a hundred-dollar bill. "I need you to go back there and get Sunni." He plucked off another one and laid both bills on the counter. "Let her know that I've been waiting and it's very important."

Trill could tell by the look in her eyes that the thought of those hundred-dollar bills being hers would make her do whatever he needed her to do. She grabbed the money off the counter. "I'ma see what I can do," she said. "Wait here." She faded to the back out of sight.

Before long, Sunni appeared. "Trill, I can't believe you showed up here," she shook her head.

"I didn't know I was supposed to come to your house," he replied. "I need to talk to you."

"Not now, I'm busy."

"Look, is there someplace private where we can go talk? I don't want everybody in our business."

"For the record, we don't have any business," she said as she turned to walk away. "But we can go into my office for a minute."

Sunni led Trill through the shop, which was packed like the welfare office. Although there was a sign that clearly read "no children allowed unless being serviced," there was a woman with a scarf on her head and a badass little boy who was ripping the pages out of the magazines. Then there was the thick chick in a hot pink, size medium velour jogging suit. Apparently, no one had told her she needed a size XL. And who could miss the dusty chick, the one so ugly no one could figure out why she would waste $55 on a cute hairdo when she would still just be a gorilla with a cute hairdo.

Once they entered Sunni's office, Trill pulled the gun from his waist and handed it to her.

"Thanks," he said. "I brought you something else, too." He put the white box he had been carrying down on her desk.

"Thank you, but I can't chitchat with you right now," Sunni replied.

"I respect your gangsta. Believe me." He moved the piece of hair from in front of her eye that had fallen down out of her doobie, admiring her natural beauty in the raw.

"I appreciate that."

"May I have a hug before I let the door hit me?"

She embraced him, and it felt good. But as she requested, he didn't take up much more of her time. Before he turned to walk away, he kissed her on the forehead and said, "Let me know when you're free so we can 'chitchat' over dinner or something."

Before both of his feet were out of the shop door good, the gossip was all through the shop and Sunni learned Trill's life story: his life before he went to prison, the night that sent him to prison, life while in the penitentiary and everything about Precious in between. At first she felt pity for Precious, but when she got the real scoop on Precious *Pay-Me,* she changed her opinion.

Ta-Ta came in on the tail end of things and added her two cents. "Girl, that bitch, Precious, ain't nothing to sleep on. I used to do Trill's baby momma first cousin's best friend's hair back in the day, and that ho Precious tricked that girl out of her baby."

"What?" Sunni questioned.

"Uha-huh, she had to make sure she had extra insurance against Trill."

"You think so."

"What person who ain't getting high gonna give their baby up willingly to a got-damn peg-leg bitch?"

"You got a point."

Hearing the various sides of gossip about Trill, all in all, Sunni liked what she heard, and especially the loyalty he had to Precious.

Before she was ready to go, Cher dropped in to see if Sunni wanted to go have drinks with her. Sunni declined, but still sat and talked to Cher for a couple minutes over a cold fish sandwich that she had ordered earlier but was too busy to eat.

"Girl, I really like this nigga. But at the same time he already got a chick, a baby and some drama."

"That ho ain't his baby momma. She's just using that baby." Cher voiced her opinion to her friend.

"I don't need no more unnecessary trouble."

"You know what? At least go and have dinner with him. Meet with him and hear what he has to say."

"I'ma think about it," Sunni said. "Thanks for stopping by. Sorry I couldn't go get drinks with you tonight. I've just worked myself to the bone and all I want is a bath and my bed."

"I'll talk to you tomorrow, gurrrll."

"Give me a few minutes to grab my pocketbook out my office and I'll walk out with you."

Sunni went to her office to grab her purse and saw the box from Trill; she had forgotten all about it. She opened up the box and immediately her heart melted. It was a yellow teddy bear wearing a bulletproof vest. The card read:

I thought long and hard of something that I could give you that would give you a better understanding of how I feel. I thought and thought and the only thing I could come up with was some gangsta mathematics:

$(L+T) \times Lty2 = DBD$

Translation:

Love plus Trust, multiplied by Loyalty (to the second power)

Equals . . .

Death Before Dishonor

If you can stand what I have to give to you then give me a call. But if you can't stand the

pressure, I know you ain't no diamond for real.
You trying to shine or what?

Trill
804-777-9311

Tears were in her eyes because that nigga had just dropped some deep shit on her. She knew she was a jewel, a diamond in the rough, and she was ready to shine. Sunni took the chip off her shoulder, picked up the phone and called Trill. She ended up getting his voice mail. *Ain't this a bitch,* she thought.

"At the sound of the beep, leave a message," the automated recording requested.

"Nine o'clock at my house. Saturday night," Sunni spoke into the phone. "It's then and there or nowhere."

The
Gangsta
Table

Scenes from the *Once Upon a Time in America* limited-edition DVD covered the 60" screen of the Phillips plasma television, but the sound was on mute. The music from Tupac Shakur's *Me Against the World* poured out of the state-of-the-art sound system. The table was solid oak and eight feet in diameter. There was a 33 x 36-inch full-color, high-resolution copy of the last photo ever taken of the late rapper embedded into the surface and the entire circumference of the table was covered by a three-quarter-inch-thick sheet of cut crystal. It was called "the gangsta table" and the business was: money, murder and mayhem.

Trill implemented the gangsta table so his crew could

feel like they were more of an organization, a Mafia—so they would take it seriously, like any organized crime ring, not just a few stickup kids.

If the table could talk, boy, the stories it would tell. Not only could the chatter from that gangsta table put the whole crew behind bars for multiple life sentences, but it could have landed them in the grave. The table could make a lot of money from the plans and info it had as well. Seventy-five percent of the executive decisions were made there. The verdict of many lives were delivered at this table: who'd fall victim, who'd live and who'd die. It was reckless how they made such decisions under the influence of a fully stocked bar and a punch bowl filled with hydro.

Everyone sat around the table and waited for the meeting to start so they could map out the blueprint of the next plan to stack more paper. Mont, Seven, Jon-Jon and Noc-Noc waited for the meeting to begin.

Trill opened, "So, Jon, what you got for us?"

Jon-Jon had a huge white box sitting on the floor by his feet; he pulled a stack of manila envelopes out of it. He went through his organized files as if he was preparing for a major presentation at a Fortune 500 company.

Taking a deep breath, he answered, "Yeah, I been on the grind."

"Nigga, you kills me with that shit. You sit at a fucking computer all day and eat bon-bons. Talkin' 'bout you on the grind," Noc-Noc interrupted.

"Let him do him and you do you," Trill said. "Everybody got a position on the team."

"Aight, give me your daily task list, nigga," Noc-Noc said with a smirk on his face.

"For starters," Jon-Jon stated, "I got bios on a few good marks, phone records and BlackBerry and text message records, and details on their moves, whereabouts, associates and dealings."

"Damn, nigga! FBI, CIA, DEA—they ain't got shit on you. We got the same shit they got." Noc-Noc was impressed.

Trill shot a look over at Noc-Noc, killing the small talk. Then he focused his attention back to Jon-Jon. "Show me what you got."

Jon-Jon placed ten 8 x 10 photos on the table. Diego was in all ten shots.

"Fernando Fuentes, aka Carlos Dominguez, bka Diego Sanchez—just a few of his many aliases," Jon-Jon reported. "He supplies more than seventy percent of the heroin in the city and fifty percent of the powder cocaine. He did two years of hard time in a South American prison." Jon-Jon then placed three mug shots on the table.

"He's originally from Cuba, grew up in Miami, but his mother and wife live in Canada." Jon-Jon put photos of the women on the table. "This is the only thing in the world he cares about."

"Damn, nigga. I'm glad we still on the same team," Trill said, which was his way of complimenting Jon-Jon's thoroughness.

Jon-Jon continued reading from the paper in front of him. "He never misses a first and third Friday with his family. That's his only routine."

"He's a no-no," Mont blurted out. "Too powerful for us to fuck with."

"Fuck that Diego punk," Noc-Noc spoke up. "That lame—"

"Let him speak," Trill cut Noc-Noc off. "Let's hear all the info before we make emotional decisions."

"He's a heartless maniac with unlimited power and money. I heard he was the devil reincarnated," Mont explained. "They say he once killed a friend of a nigga who owed him a hundred dollars on a bet!"

"I don't fear no motherfucker," Noc-Noc boasted.

Jon-Jon nodded, "I agree, but I will need more time to further study him."

"You got that?" Trill said. "We gon' put him on ice for now. Who else do you have?"

"That's the thing," Jon-Jon said. "I need more time to gather more shit on his generals. They are all people he brought in with him." Jon-Jon could read everybody's expressions. Before Noc-Noc started to speak, Jon-Jon put his hand up. "But, but—hold your horses, young gun," he said. "But most of the lieutenants are local cats. And believe me, they holding, too."

Jon-Jon laid another picture out. "In my opinion, this would be a real prosperous and quick lick. His name is Roderick Logan but he likes to be called Ricardo Lacks since he's down with Diego now." Everybody studied the photo as Jon-Jon began to give them the rundown. "He's a easy mark, if it's done right. This dude is a lil' youngun, gets a lot of money and needs to be taught a lesson simply because he's sloppy and careless."

"Good, I'm ready to go take a lot of money," Noc-Noc said.

Jon-Jon nodded in agreement. "Evidently nobody really taught youngun the game. And if we don't get him, the police will."

Trill spoke. "I think I got an idea comin' on for him."

"Good," Jon-Jon said. "He's what I feel is the easiest target, along with a couple of others that I have in-depth files on as well."

After Trill and his crew finished mapping everything

out, Trill checked his voice mail and heard the message Sunni had left for him. Once he hung up, he had a puzzled smile on his face.

"What's up, cuz?" Noc-Noc asked.

"Nothing, man," Trill answered. "Just been a change of plans. We gon' move the time up a bit earlier. We gon' make it seven," Trill informed everybody. "But we gon' meet up at three to go over e'rything one more time."

"It's still going to be light outside," Mont protested.

"Nigga, you think Castro's soldiers tell him that they can't go to war because it's light outside? This meeting is over," Trill announced.

With that being said, everything was everything, everybody knew what the game plan was and what position needed to be played.

Strong-Arming

rill, Mont, Jon-Jon, and Seven sat in the Hertz rental van, Trill with binoculars zeroed in on the mark's house. There was minimum activity going on until around 6:30 P.M., just like Jon-Jon said there would be.

"Roderick out at 6:30 P.M. to pick his girlfriend up from work and then at 10:00 P.M. to hit the block," Jon-Jon had told them. "That leaves only his grandparents in the house."

After Roderick left to go pick up his girl, Trill suggested that they wait about thirty minutes in case he doubled back. They would be in and out in a flash providing everything went accordingly. Once an unenthused Noc-Noc made the call informing the crew that Ricardo had arrived at his girlfriend's job, they put their plan in motion. Things seemed kinda strange without Noc-Noc being there on the heist. However, it had to be that way because this was supposed to be nonviolent, and Noc-Noc was too trigger-happy.

Trill gave the order. "Let's do this shit." He looked at Jon-Jon to make his move. Jon-Jon used his laptop to disable the phone lines inside the house. He put his hat and jacket on, hopped out of the rental van and approached the front door of Roderick's house. *I hope this goes as planned, I'd hate for one of these old-timers to get hurt,* he thought, as he knocked on the door.

A little old lady in a flowery housecoat with snaps on it and pink sponge rollers in her hair answered the door.

"Yes, young man," she said, "can I help you?" The old lady looked at Jon-Jon curiously.

"Mrs. Agnes Logan?" Jon-Jon said as he smelled the aroma of chicken being fried.

"Yes." She peered at him over her bifocal glasses.

"My name is Ralph Langhorne." He flashed a fake badge. "I am with the Drug Enforcement Agency."

She looked at his hat that read "DEA" and glanced at the badge. "Yes," she said, waiting for him to continue.

"I need to speak to you."

"For what? I don't use any drugs, sonny."

Jon-Jon laughed. "I know you don't, Mrs. Logan. May I come in? I just want to talk to you. I don't want to bring any attention to your house."

"Well, uh . . . come in." She opened up the door and motioned for him to come inside.

"Agnes, who is it?" an elderly man's voice called from the back part of the house.

"Walter, cut that chicken off for me."

"Okay, but who is it?"

"It's a policeman. He want to talk to me," she said in a scratchy voice that had been around for many seasons.

"Don't let him in," Walter called out.

"I would like to talk to you, too, sir," Jon-Jon spoke up.

Walter Logan entered the room. "Do you have a warrant?" he asked.

"No, sir," Jon-Jon said in a firm tone. "Like I said, I just want to talk."

"Well, if you ain't got no got-damn warrant, get the hell out of my got-damn house," Walter huffed.

"Walter, don't talk to the man like that. All that cussing ain't necessary. You know God don't like ugly."

"No, sir. I don't have a warrant, but I can get one," Jon-Jon lied. "I was hoping that I wouldn't have to. Your grandson said you would cooperate."

"Roderick?" Agnes cried out. "Ohhh, Lord."

"Yes, he's being detained," Jon-Jon said, "and we're here to retrieve the money. We've confiscated the drugs. He said that you, Mrs. Logan, were holding a large sum of money for him. I don't want to take you in but I will if I have to," Jon-Jon bluffed, but his heart started racing when he saw two shotguns in the corners of the room.

"No, I'm too old to go to jail," she pleaded.

"I agree, and I don't want to take you. So, let's keep this simple, okay?"

She looked off into space and didn't speak, waiting to see what Jon-Jon wanted with them.

In a calm voice, he asked, "How much of your grandson's money would you say you have in your possession?"

She hesitated. "Uhh," she began to stutter.

Jon-Jon could see her mind roaming, in search of a lie. "Mrs. Logan, it's very important that you tell the truth to the best of your knowledge."

"About nine hundred thousand the last time I counted," she blurted out.

"Nine *hundred* thousand?" Grandpa Walter jumped in. "Is you fucking crazy, Agnes? You told me it was about nine thousand. Woman, is you fucking out yo' mind?"

"Walter, don't talk to me like that. Don't cuss at me, Walter," Agnes replied with teary eyes.

"You're going to have to tell me where the money is in order for me to offer you immunity," Jon-Jon said, still very much in character.

Jon-Jon saw Grandpa eyeing the shotgun beside the china cabinet. He reached for his walkie-talkie and began speaking. "This is Agent Longhorne on Double Blue. The perimeter is secure except two shotguns in the dining room area of the house. Mrs. Logan has agreed to cooperate." The front door opened and Trill, Mont and Seven entered. "These are my colleagues. I wanted to talk to you before they came in because at times they are not as nice as I am."

"Them?" Walter said, pointing to the crew. "Them ain't no got-damn DEA agents. This shit is a motherfucking setup!"

Agnes looked up and quickly studied the men in her house. She believed what her husband was saying was true. She was more comfortable with the possibility of being imprisoned than being in the hands of these gangsters.

She looked the thugs over, each was carrying an MP-5. She went Miss Celie from *The Color Purple* on them and put up her two fingers like she was about to hex someone.

"The devil is a liar," she began to preach. "Devil, I rebuke you in the name of Jesus." All of a sudden, even though she was scared to death, she got all sanctified.

"Look, Grandma, you know what we came for, so give it up," Mont instructed her.

"Agnes, go on ahead and give them the money," Walter advised her. "They got machine guns, so go on ahead and give them what they came fo'."

"No weapon formed against me shall prosper. And you," Agnes said to Jon-Jon, "tricking an old woman like me. You going straight to hell. All you demons going to hell." She pointed at each and every one of them with a glare in her eyes. "You gon' burn in hell! You hear me?"

"Grandma, these guys ain't nice like me," Jon-Jon warned her. "They will kill you and your husband, so please give them the money."

"Yea, though I walk through the valley of the shadow of death," Agnes prayed out loud, "I will fear no evil, for Thou art with me."

Seven picked up a vase and threw it against the wall, startling Agnes, and when she saw Trill holding a gun to Walter's head, she was scared shitless. "The devil is a liar. God is my source and protector!" Seven held his gun up and put the red beam on her housecoat. "But I'm going to give you this money." She looked at Seven. "Make yo'self

DEATH BEFORE DISHONOR

useful and come and get this thing with the money in it."
She led the way, both Seven and Jon-Jon following behind her. She moved so quickly that the fellas could see
the top of her knee-highs. She continued her prayer. "The
Lord is my shepherd. I shall not want." She strode down
the hall. "And didn't yo' momma teach you about the Ten
Commandments? Thou shalt not steal?"

Agnes led Seven into her bedroom, where the money
was. On the way, they walked through the kitchen and
Seven couldn't resist the chicken sitting on the counter.
He picked up a breast and took a bite. "Damn, Grandma,
you sho' can cook!"

Once they entered her bedroom, she pointed to the
closet. Seven and Jon-Jon got the money, which was piled
nicely in a storage container, and took it out to the van.
Once they saw the money, the others exited the house as
well.

"God don't like ugly," Agnes yelled out to the street,
waving her fist, "and you gon' see this again on Judgment Day!"

The four men pulled away from the curb about a million dollars richer. They would deal with Judgment Day
when that day came.

Caught Slipping

*A*fter the heist, Trill rushed home to get ready for his other business for the night. He only had enough time to go to the house to take a shower and change his clothes so that he would be on time for his date with Sunni.

"I missed you, baby," Precious greeted Trill as he walked through the door.

"Yeah, me, too," he said, heading into the kitchen. He put a bag down on the table that contained his cut of the money.

"You in for the night?" Precious asked.

"Nope, I got to go meet somebody."

"Is it business?" As always her mind was on money.

He didn't answer her; instead he made his way to his

son's room. "Where's Lil' Trill?" he asked once he entered the bedroom and saw that his baby boy wasn't in there.

"He's staying over at his friend's house tonight. I was supposed to be going out with Molly for dinner, but I can cancel and chill with you. It can be just you and me," she suggested as Trill walked out of the room and went into the bathroom. But Trill had other plans.

"I gotta drive a ways out, so I'll be back late most likely," he said as he stood over the toilet pissing; he didn't know what Sunni had up her sleeve. Precious stood in the doorway. After he finished using the toilet, he reached to turn the shower on. "I'll holla at you when I get out of the shower," he said as he pushed the door shut, leaving a crack.

"I'll be waitin'," she said in a jolly voice. "I'll be in there in a lil' while to kick it wit' you."

Trill cut the radio in the shower on and turned the volume up high. He waited a minute and then tiptoed out of the bathroom and headed down to the kitchen. Still fully dressed he burst in the kitchen, yelling, "Bitch, what the fuck you doing?"

Precious jumped, dropping the money she had just taken out of the bag onto the floor. She knew she had been caught red-handed.

Trill had finally caught her doing something that she had been doing ever since his very first heist after coming home from prison. At first he thought he had just miscounted by a few hundred—but then the amounts started going from hundreds to a couple thousand. As much as he gave Precious everything she desired, he just couldn't allow himself to think that she was actually stealing from him, stealing what could have been hers if she had only asked. He had to set the trap to be sure.

"I was just moving the money off the table while I cleaned it off," she said, allowing the quickest lie that she could think of to roll off her tongue.

"You's a fucking thief!" Trill yelled, moving closer to her face. He could hear her heart beat out of control from fear of not knowing what he would do next.

"Baby, how could you think . . ."

"No, bitch, why didn't you think? You thought I wouldn't figure this shit out."

"Trill, I swear I—"

"Don't," Trill said, holding his hand up to stop her in the midst of her lying. "You know this shit right here is the ultimate act of disrespect and disloyalty. I'ma need some time to think. I'm out. I'll deal with you later," he said, picking up his money.

Trill headed back upstairs to his bedroom, leaving

Precious to drown in her own tearful lies. He grabbed his clothes and decided he'd take a shower over at Sunni's and then he left out the house. Under normal circum- stances he would have been hurt, but in a way he was relieved. Lately, observing Precious' reckless spending, he was beginning to think that in order to maintain her, he would have to keep robbing and hustling for the rest of his life.

12

Niggas
and Flies

$\mathcal{A}$fter Diego got the phone call from Ricardo that his grandma had just been robbed, Diego was fuming. All fingers pointed to them, everything was too mapped out for it to not be an inside job. Diego knew what he had to do: kill Ricardo and Agnes.

Agnes looked out the window and saw three big extended black Denalis pull up in front of her house. She watched as a load of gangstas exited the trucks, and Diego got out wearing a green leather outfit.

"What all dese goons coming in here for?" she asked Ricardo. Ricardo was on pins and needles, sweat pouring from his forehead. He had a glass of Hennessey in his hand and put it down to talk to his grandmother. Ricardo, the spitting image of his grandfather, looked like he couldn't be any more than sixteen even though he was twenty.

"Look, Nanna," Ricardo said, "you gotta talk to my boss."

"Yo' boss? Since when did you have a job?"

"Nanna, fo' real, these people ain't nothing to play with. I'm in big trouble."

"No, baby," she said with such ease, "you would rather deal with them than with me." She had her broom in her hand and she raised it at him. "I ought to knock you out, putting me up to keeping that money for you."

"I know, Nanna. I'm guilty and I was wrong and you can get me for that later," he said. She could see the fear in his eyes. "But right now you gotta tell them everything that happened or else—" He was interrupted by a knock at the door.

Walter sat quietly in the corner with two pistols under the cushions of his chair. Ricardo answered the door. Agnes walked into the kitchen and begin singing a chant. Ricardo led Diego to the kitchen. "Grandma, this is my friend, tell him what happened."

Diego motioned for Ricardo and his goons to leave him alone with Agnes in the kitchen. He looked around and then his eyes met hers.

"What happen?" he snapped at her.

"Honey, sit down," she said calmly. "You want Nanna to make you some hot cocoa?"

Raising his voice, he demanded, "No, I want to know where the fuck is my money?" He hit the table with the bottom of his fist.

"Well, you don't have to be so hostile with me. I done already took one nerve pill, I don't need to take another one." She looked into Diego's eyes like only a mother can do a son. "I understand you're upset but maybe you need one. Do you want one?" she asked, walking to the cabinet to pull out her bottle of Valium.

"I don't need no pills." He lowered his voice. "Just tell me what happen."

"Well, let's see," she said as she rubbed her chin and then began to pace the kitchen floor, "it was about twenty of them and they had oozies and smoozies. They came in here being disrespectful to me." She grabbed her heart and whispered, "They scared me half to death. You know an old woman like me can't take too much."

"Tell me why I shouldn't kill you and your son?" Diego didn't cut any corners.

She gazed at him. "Why would you? I already took care of that guy who got the money."

Diego shook his head in disbelief, wondering to himself why this old woman was bullshitting him and why he didn't kill her right then and there.

"You took care of them?" he asked with a slight chuckle, wondering how long this old woman would continue this foolish talk.

"Yes, I was in the middle of taking care of it, but Ricardo and Walter, they made me stop because I had to clean up that mess they made since you was coming."

"Stop what?" he asked. "You got them tied up in the backyard or sumthin' I don't know about?"

She smiled. "Better than that."

"You got his balls on a platter?" Diego joked.

"Oh, you want to help Granny finish this hooligan off? I'ma teach him a lesson about robbing old people," she said. "Now you in or you gon' sit there with your lips poked out crying over some spilled milk?" She grabbed the piece of chicken that Seven had bit off and left behind.

Diego's first thought was to grab the butcher knife on the cabinet and cut her throat but for some reason he hesitated. Then she asked, "You got a handkerchief? I got work to do. I need something of yours to wrap that little thief's bones in, teach him about messing with Grandma Agnes' babies. Don't nobody mess with my cheerrens."

Diego plastered a big smile on his face; being Cuban, he knew all about Santeria.

He went into his pocket and handed Grandma Agnes the handkerchief. He watched as she placed the chicken bone inside and begin to chant, "Niggas and flies, both I despise! The more I'm around niggas, the more I like flies."

Diego laughed.

"Quiet," Agnes ordered. She said a chant in another language, and began to tie the edges of the handkerchief together and then tied a tight knot. Diego knew she meant business when she lit the candles and continued to chant in a strange tongue for another ten minutes.

She then proceeded to the backyard and buried the handkerchief with the bone in it, all the while singing the strange melody. All of a sudden there was silence. She sat there in complete silence for a few minutes before she got up. Diego was watching from the back door. He stood there, proud of his newest and eldest soldier. She walked back through the door "That thieving-ass heathen ain't gon' have no good luck! You mark my word."

Diego didn't know what to say. He only looked at her and for a brief second he felt like he was looking into his own grandmother's eyes, back in Cuba.

"Now come on and give Grandma Agnes a hug," she

said. "You know Grandma is always here for you anytime you need me."

She had somehow done what many had set out to do many times and failed: reach Diego's heart.

Diego nodded and gave her a quick hug, not wanting anyone to see the soft side of him. As he exited the kitchen, everybody was sitting around nervously waiting for their next command. He looked at Ricardo. "I'm going to promote you tomorrow. Come and see me bright and early."

Deigo stopped to use the bathroom and then left the house with his entourage following him. As they drove away, Ricardo fell to his knees, thanking God for allowing him to live to see another day.

Toe
to Toe

"This is the tenth time I have called this nigga, and he ain't answered the fucking phone not once," Precious informed her best friend, Molly, as they waited for a table at the Cheesecake Factory.

She slammed the flip phone shut holding it tight in her hand, wishing it would ring. She was terrified that Trill had caught her red-handed and needed to talk to him to figure out where his head was.

"Girl, he probably working." Molly tried to ease her best friend's mind.

"Fuck that! I don't give a shit. I am so tired of hustling-ass niggas always acting like they working."

"A nigga like Trill gotta work to take care of yo' high-maintenance ass."

"You right, but still." Precious changed the subject and directed her attention to the hostess. "How long before the table for Pay is ready?"

"Just one more minute, ma'am. They're cleaning it off now," the hostess informed Precious.

"Girl, they need to hurry the fuck on," Precious complained. "My feet are hurting in these Manolos."

"You mean your foot," her friend since middle school reminded her.

"Whatever." Precious pouted as she sucked her teeth and put her hand on her hip.

"Right this way," the hostess announced.

As soon as they were seated, Precious dialed Trill's number again. "This motherfucker still ain't answering my call."

"Precious, I wasn't gon' tell you, but I heard that Trill was at Sunny Delight hollering at the owner. Say he was pressed and some mo' shit," Molly then turned her attention to the menu, not wanting to see the look on Precious' face after breaking the news to her. And even more so, she didn't want Precious to be able to see the smirk she was trying to hold back.

"The owner?" Precious asked.

"Yeah, her name is Sunni."

"Oh, her, she ain't nobody. See that's how rumors get started. She a chick that, ummm, Noc-Noc be hollering at." Precious was mad as hell, but she didn't want Molly to have anything up on her when it came to Trill.

"You sure? Because I heard Trill was up there, begging to see her."

"Yeah, I'm . . ." Precious was at a loss. Steam started coming out of her head because she knew for certain that she had fucked up now. Trill was in a vulnerable state, and if there wasn't anything going on between him and this Sunni chick before, the odds of there being something going on after tonight was a definite possibility. He was probably with Sunni now. "Who is this Sunni, anyway? Do you know her?" Precious cleaned it up, acting as if maybe there was another Sunni that she had gotten mixed up with.

"Like you said, she ain't nobody, just a bitch that owns an all-night beauty salon."

Precious dialed Trill again and got no answer; it went straight to voice mail. "When you need to know what is going on," Precious fumed, "like my momma always said, go to the root of the problem." With that being said, Precious picked up the phone and called information. "Yes, give me the number to Sunny Delight."

Once she got the number, she called the shop look- ing for Sunni. In between rings she vented to Molly, "Oh, best believe I am going to get to the bottom of this."

"Thank you for calling Sunny Delight," the receptionist answered the phone, "where it's bright and sunny. How may I help you?"

"Just put Sunni on the phone," Precious demanded.

Ta-Ta, who had just walked into the shop and was standing there talking to the receptionist when the phone rang, motioned for the phone after reading the Caller ID, "Precious Pay." Ta-Ta grinned, took the phone from the receptionist and said, "Yeah, what you need with Sunni?"

"Look, is this Sunni? If not, you need to put her on the motherfucking phone, okay?"

"Hold on." Ta-Ta knew it was going to be a long night, and she lived for this kind of drama. There was no need for any Red Bull, Vivarin or No-Doz. It would be this phone conversation that would get her through the night. "Yes, can I help you?" she said, changing her voice up, trying hard to sound like Sunni.

"Look, what's going on with you and Trill?" Precious said, getting right to the point.

"Who is this?"

"It's his wife! Now, bitch, answer the question."

"First of all, you need to calm down. Secondly, why are you calling me at *my* job about *your* husband?"

"Bitch, don't play with me. I'll come up and beat yo' ass."

"What? You gon' take your fake leg off and try to beat me with it?"

"I ain't got to. Bitch, we can go at it toe to toe."

"Toe to toe? You are short a few of those, ain't cha . . . ho?"

Ta-Ta laughed hysterically as Precious screamed, "What's so funny? Ain't shit funny, bitch! Not a damn thing. You don't know me."

"Oh, you mean you ain't that one-legged ho from *The Sopranos* that Tony was fuckin'? Tell me, how does a one-legged chick wrap her legs around her man? Oh, that's right, she doesn't. She dreams about it." Once again, Ta-Ta burst out laughing.

"So you still think shit is funny?"

"You right. It ain't funny, is it?" Ta-Ta walked over and hit the CD player's On button and turned up the volume. Lady Sal sang, "I got yo' man and you can't do anything about it."

Precious had heard enough. "Bitch, when I see you, it's on!"

"It's on then, you peg-leg ho. But by the way, this ain't even Sunni! Take this quarter and play yo'self, bee-yotch!" Ta-Ta hung up the phone as everyone in the shop fell out laughing.

Real Talk

nce Trill arrived at Sunni's house, he parked in the driveway and went and knocked on her door. Sunni opened the door and greeted Trill with a hug. "It's good to see you." Sunni smiled. "How was your day?"

"Honestly"—he took a deep breath—"it was a bit rocky. A real long day."

"Sorry to hear that it wasn't all that great. Do you want to tell me all about it?" she asked as she invited him in.

"It comes wit' the territory. You gotta take the bad wit' the good. All I need is a shower, some good company from you and some rest and I'll be good."

"I can manage that," Sunni assured him.

Something about Sunni's spirit made him feel relaxed. He didn't feel the need to be on guard all the time. Although her house wasn't half as extravagant as his and Precious', it was more than a house. It was a home.

"Are you hungry? You want something to eat?" Sunni asked.

"I'm starving." Trill watched Sunni walk toward the kitchen in her Seven jeans and her teal shirt that revealed one of her shoulders. He was no longer sure just exactly what he was hungry for—food or Sunni.

"I can warm up some of this lasagna I cooked last night."

"I'll pass on the lasagna. My momma always told me not to eat a woman's lasagna or spaghetti."

"She told you right, but I promise you"—she looked in his eyes—"I'm not trying to work no roots on you. I'm not interested in keeping no man who don't want to be kept. You feel me?"

"I feel that." Trill nodded. "I do want something to eat, but I want us to go out so we can talk. I want to know who Sunni is, the woman under all that armor."

"Since you're tired, how about we just chill inside and order in. We can sit by the fireplace and chat there," Sunni suggested.

"Only if you agree to participate and give me a heart to heart."

"Just make sure you keep it real," she informed him as she went up the stairs to draw his bathwater.

It was taking a few minutes for Sunni to get things together for Trill in the bathroom, so, he got up from the sofa and went upstairs, to check on her.

"Hey, where you at?" he called as he roamed the hall.

"I'm in here," Sunni yelled out from the bathroom.

"What you doin'?" he said as he entered.

"I'm getting everything straight so I can give you a bath, a massage and a pedicure since you had a long day."

"Are you going to personally bathe me?"

"I can." She smiled.

"That's a good look."

"Yeah, just make sure you return the favor when I have a bad day," Sunni returned with a wink as she tested the temperature of the water with her hand.

"No doubt."

"Well, everything you need is in here," Sunni said as she exited the bathroom.

"Not anymore," Trill hinted.

"I'll be waiting right outside the door for you," Sunni said, then smiled and walked away. "Holler when you're undressed and in the water."

Within a few minutes Sunni responded to Trill's call that he was ready for her to come wash his back. As she did so, Trill began asking her about her life.

"Why don't you have a man? I know you like what we got," Trill said with a laugh as her hand dipped down over his belly.

"That's a long story."

"I got time."

"Okay, but remember you asked. I was with this dude, Scoop. Not living with him. I was living with my gram. Scoop made the mistake of selling coke to a snitch right on the front porch. When the police kicked in the door, it went flying off the hinges, and my grandmother had a heart attack right then and there."

Trill looked at her sympathetically.

"I won't never forgive Scoop for that. But then it got worse. Gram's health got worse after that, and she died. She was the only dependable and stable thing I ever had in my life. Scoop comes along saying he's gonna take care of me."

Sunni shook her head, remembering how Scoop nobly stepped up to the plate and vowed that he would take care of her, that he would make sure she always had a roof over her head and a full belly. He vowed that he would be everything that she ever needed in a man. The Bible says better it is that thou shouldest not vow, than that thou shouldest vow and not pay. Well, obviously Scoop's grandmother never dragged his butt to church.

"Yeah, and what happened?" Trill wanted to know.

"When the indictments came out, Scoop found out that he was facing twenty years. Until death do us part, ride or die, death before dishonor to anybody, including his momma, went clean out of the window. He cracked at the pickup. Before he was even sitting down good in the interrogation room, not only had he given up all his peoples, but me, too."

"Some niggas." Trill shook his head.

It didn't matter that Sunni had never touched a drug a day in her life. She didn't even know cocaine from baby powder. The detectives didn't give a shit. Somebody had to take the charge. Since Sunni didn't cooperate with the detectives by providing them with the information they needed when they were trying to pin the case on Scoop, she would have to do some time. It didn't matter if she had showed up to court dressed like a nun, she was still going straight to hell if the system had anything to do with it.

"So that's how you wound up in the penitentiary?"

"At nineteen years old, I was sentenced to five years. Got out after three for good behavior."

"How did you manage to do so well when you got out?"

"While I was locked up, I got my GED. I also got certificates in cosmetology and business management. Most important, I learned how to manipulate the system. My gram was my inspiration; Scoop was, too, in a way, because I promised myself I would never let anyone do me that way again."

After the bath was over, the Chinese food arrived and they sat in front of the fireplace and continued to enjoy the company of one another.

"So, what's up with you and that girl Precious?" Sunni just came out and asked. It was his turn to 'fess up.

Trill was about to come up with a lie, but decided to shoot from the hip, keeping it totally real. "Honestly, I'm trying to figure that out myself. Everything ain't everything like I thought it was. As you know, sometimes that same person we put all of our trust in is the one who should be the least trusted."

"Amen," Sunni agreed.

"I just need to figure a few things out."

"Well, let's figure them out together," Sunni said, moving in closer, giving Trill her undivided attention.

"Precious was someone who I used to fuck and used as an arm piece before I got locked up. I was a mediocre hustler, getting money on a way smaller scale than I am now." Sunni listened attentively as Trill continued. "Anyway, we were out one night and some bustas tried to rob me. I think they thought because I was out with a chick that I wasn't gon' have a piece on me. But they was dead wrong, I never leave home without it."

"That's why you were giving me such a hard time about you not having your pistol."

He nodded and continued with his confession. "Well, I was shooting back on the strength. She got caught in the cross fire and ended up losing her leg."

"No way." Sunni felt kind of bad that she had to act as if she didn't already know the business. "Damn!"

"Once I went to jail, Shawdy held me down. She raised my son for me. To this day I don't even know how she held it down, fo' real."

"That's deep."

"Witnessing her do all that for me"—he dropped his head—"I fell in love with her. I really had no other choice but to give her my undying love and loyalty."

"I feel that," Sunni said, but Trill could see the disappointment in her eyes.

Trill caressed her face with the back of his hand. "But a lot has changed and now the stakes are different."

"How so?"

"They just are."

"I don't understand. Can you please make me understand? Because I am about to put my shield back up and the armor is going back on."

He put his hand up and said, "Hold up! Hear me out."

"I'm listening."

"Look, I've been hustling in the streets since I was 'bout fourteen, knowing firsthand illegal hustling got a time capsule on it." Sunni looked at Trill as he continued to drop jewels on her. "Once I was released from prison, my plan was to come home and build a foundation for us, a house, nice cars, work on getting a business, stack me some real paper and get out the game."

"Sounds like you had a pretty good plan. What happened?"

"Usually a plan consists of a few good men or women."

"Oh?"

"Well, I put my work in, but Shawdy girl, she . . ." He shook his head as his words tapered off.

Inside Sunni got a bit enthusiastic, but she didn't show it. Her round eyes focused in on him like a puppy dog.

"You know how dudes come home from the penitentiary and they try to play catch-up?" Trill voiced, staring off as if he were reminiscing.

Death Before Dishonor

Sunni nodded. "I've seen it a many of times."

"Well, it was vice versa. She wanted to play catch-up.

Needed a house off the bat. Within two months of me coming home, I bought our house, a house she had clipped out a magazine."

"Wow! You hit the ground running."

"Got her a nice whip, the finest prosthetic leg money could buy and I gave her an allowance every week. I'm not bragging. Nor am I kicking dirt on Shawdy, either. I just felt like I owed that to her, you know."

Sunni assured him that she understood. She was engrossed in the conversation because she had never had such a real conversation with a man. She was used to lies and deceit.

"No matter how much I gave her, it was never enough. And never did she try to move forward with the business ventures we talked about to make us legit."

"That's crazy to me. I wish I had someone who could have given me a jump start on my business."

"How did you get your business?" Trill probed, turning the tables.

"When I came home from jail, I still had money that Scoop had given me to put away early in our relationship. I gave it to my friend Cher to hold for me. I didn't know she was still going to have it when I came home. After all

I had been through, I was sure it would be gone."

"Damn, Cher is a real soldier."

"Fa'real." Then Sunni changed the subject back to him. "So you gon' marry Precious?"

"Like I said, I appreciate everything she's done and I will always hold her down. But on some real shit, it ain't no future there. I'm trying to retire and have a legit business." There was silence between them. He took her hand into his and looked at her. "Real talk, from the heart." He put his hand on his heart. "I haven't been this comfortable with a woman in a long time. Never even thought I could feel this way."

"Straight like that?" Sunni asked softly.

"Straight like that."

Fallen
Soldiers

The two-story house, the only house that was occupied on the run-down street, was the next hit. The neighborhood was the Sugar Bottom District and wasn't shit sweet about it. Only the living dead resided and roamed the streets there. The area was infested with rats the size of possum, stray malnourished dope fiends, winos and two-bit crack whores. Although the dilapidated community rested between historic Church Hill and Fulton Hill, more than eighty percent of the city's residents had never ventured to the area. The police had unofficially washed their hands of the place. Which made it the perfect place for a pharmaceutical purveyor to set up shop. From the outside, it looked like the house would crumble if the wind blew hard enough. But on the inside, one of Diego's biggest drug enterprises was going strong.

For the past two weeks, Jon-Jon had disguised himself to look as dirty and smell as funky as the inhabitants of the environment around him. He fit in well as he stood over the raggedy trash barrel where a fire blazed. This was all that some of the permanent residents of the neighborhood had as a means of heat during the winter. Jon-Jon had made this his home away from home for the last couple of weeks. He spent a lot of time pretending to be a wino while gathering info by listening to the fiends and watching the traffic and shift of soldiers change at the house. This was going to be a major takedown and they all would be paid handsomely for Jon-Jon's ingenuity. They didn't expect much resistance since Jon-Jon had only seen two men on the shift that they planned to attack. Hell, they had done more for less in the past. This was going to be as sweet as a virgin's pussy with a bowl of cherries.

The hardest part was actually getting inside the house because Diego had it on lock. It was almost like a mini Fort Knox: reinforced steel doors and bars on the windows. At the gangsta table they explored their limited options. Trill decided that they couldn't be forceful and kick in the door because the door wasn't going to budge. They couldn't knock on the door; Trill was certain that Diego had trained his boys better than that. But the fortress did have one weakness: a small window in the basement. For days in the wee hours of the mornings, little by little, Seven and Noc-Noc tampered with the bars on that window until it was finally ajar. Now they waited until it was time to put the scheme into motion.

Before the kickoff, Jon-Jon buddied up with the lost souls that he had met while hovering over the fire.

"My man, look what I found," Jon-Jon said to the fiends as he opened up his filthy hands and showed a plastic baggie half-filled with little packages of heroin. He watched their eyes come to life. "You got some moonshine?" one of the drunks asked.

The fiends flocked to Jon-Jon as he passed out the packets, and one of them asked, "Where you find that?"

"One of dem, they dropped it when they got out they car." Jon-Jon pointed in the direction of the drug house.

The curious fiend wanted to know if there was more where that came from, but for now he fed his addiction. Meanwhile, a young prostitute slowly walked toward Jon-Jon smiling from ear to ear, attempting to sweet-talk Jon-Jon out of another packet of the addictive drug. It didn't take long for the drug dependent derelicts to start nodding off into their false reality with slobber drooling from their mouths. Jon-Jon shook his head and watched as one of the winos found the bottle of Wild Irish Rose that he had planted earlier. Jon-Jon smiled as he watched the wino wander off to share it with his friends. The drunks and dope fiends were so greedy that they had no idea that it was all laced. With the dope fiends all high, it was certain that there would be little to no witnesses who could get in the way of what was about to go down.

After making their way through the basement window, Trill, Seven, Noc-Noc and Mont crept up the stairs to confront their prey. Dressed in camouflage from head to toe, they made their way around the corner of the staircase until they could see the two men in plain view at a the table with a triple beam scale, weighing out the product. One was 6'2" and heavyset with a big birthmark covering a quarter of his face. The other, in dreads, was dark-skinned with a mouth full of gold teeth. He was pulling on a humongous blunt as he bagged up the hard white.

Trill smiled when he thought just how good life was. Mont's nature got hard just thinking about all that work that was going to be theirs, and he'd be the one flooding the streets of Richmond with it.

Once Trill gave the nod, everything went into action as if they were filming a trailer for the next action movie.

Before they even knew it, both workers were at gunpoint. "Lay the fuck down," Noc-Noc ordered. "And keep your hands where I can see 'em."

Trill saw the look in Birthmark's eyes and said, "Nigga, don't be no fucking fool. You guaranteed not to live through this if you try something stupid. Now follow fucking instructions."

Both men followed suit and lay down on the floor. Just when Mont was about to put the duct tape on their wrists and ankles, gunshots roared out of nowhere. Birthmark tried to take advantage of the situation and made a run for it. Noc-Noc caught him dead center in the back of the head with two slugs from his Desert Eagle. Everybody ran for cover. The initial gunshots had come from upstairs. What Trill and his assassins didn't know was that starting today, Diego had brought in extra help.

Noc-Noc caught a hot one to the arm but never stopped sparking back. If it was war they wanted, then war they would get.

Trill was behind the kitchen wall, assessing the whole scene, concentrating on where the shots were coming from. There were no other entries besides the front door and no windows. Then he noticed movement at the top of the steps. Trill couldn't tell if it was one or two men upstairs at first, he'd thought it was two guys. The shooter strategically popped in and out trying to shield himself from getting hit. Trill knew he had fucked up because when they first entered the house, he should have assigned someone to make sure that the rest of the house was empty. But Jon-Jon was never wrong.

Mont watched as a slug banged Seven in the stomach, sending him to the ground. Mont wasn't sure if that would be the bullet that would end Seven's life, but the shock sent him into a daze after seeing Seven drop to the floor. A bullet skimming his head brought him back to reality, though—making him understand that it was fight or die. Mont cocked his gun back and began gunning like his life depended on it, and it did. A bullet from Mont's gun caught Dreads in the leg as he was trying to escape out the door. It slowed him up, but Dreads still made it out or so he thought anyway.

"Go get dat nigga," Noc-Noc yelled to Mont, who was the closest to the door. "What the fuck is wrong with you?" Mont just stood there.

Once Dreads hit the outdoors, he began to run for the border. He hadn't expected to be greeted with a hot ball straight to the temple. Jon-Jon had never been in a fight in his life, let alone a gunfight. Although he wasn't born into this gangsta shit, he was sworn into it. Something had gone wrong, his friends were under a surprise attack and he felt it was his fault. Tears were in his eyes as he approached the house with his gun still smoking. His heart was racing and adrenaline was flowing. He took a deep breath, said a brief prayer, raised his gun and entered the house, ready for war.

Bleeding profusely from his left arm, Noc-Noc picked up the gun that Birthmark was originally going for and with his good arm trained pistol on the shooter upstairs and cut loose. While Noc-Noc was wilding out, Trill had moved to the side of the steps and focused in on his target, who was focusing on Noc-Noc. Trill slid his hand through the rail and took the final target down with a barrage of shots from his assault rifle. The bullets exploded the shooter's skull into fragments before riddling through the rest of his body.

When the shooting stopped, Mont joined Jon-Jon, kneeling by Seven. "You aight?" Mont asked Seven.

Jon-Jon was applying pressure to Seven's wound.

Mont called out to Trill, "We need to get these niggas some help, get them to a hospital."

"Naw, man, I'm good. We ain't leaving until we get what the fuck we came here for," Seven said, completely alert but clearly hurt.

"I'll call Dr. Moore and have him meet us at a safe spot. No hospitals, right?" Jon-Jon asked.

Trill agreed, focusing more on the situation at hand. He searched through the rest of the house to make sure that there'd only been one shooter upstairs. There was no one else there and time was of the essence. They needed to find the money and get the fuck out of there.

Mont glanced at Noc-Noc and noticed that blood was coming through his shirt. "Noc been hit, too," Mont said.

As Noc-Noc took flight to ransack the house for the money, he said, "Naw, man, my shit's good. Give me a Band-Aid and a few of them OxyContins and shit gon' be aight."

"I'ma grab this shit up right here," Mont said, pointing to the drugs on the table.

Trill spotted two kitchen-size white trash cans in the bedroom and started to smile. When he opened up the trash cans he knew that he had his eyes on his retirement funds.

16

Wanted
Dead or Alive

Diego paced the floor, as he spoke to Lee. "Nobody knows nothing?" he screamed. "I tired of this shit!" He grabbed his face then balled his fists up. "My fucking brother-in-law is *dead!*" With tears in his eyes, he asked, "How am I going to tell my wife that her little brother is coming home in pieces in a body bag and I have no explanation why?" Diego shook his head from side to side. "No more! Someone has to die."

Lee knew not to say anything. He could only imagine how Diego felt. Diego had called his brother-in-law in when things started getting hot. It was his first day on the job and now he was dead. Lee knew better than to comment at this point.

"Four of my spots hit in less than three months,"

Diego yelled. "Three million in cash, and almost a million in drugs and don't nobody know *nothing*? When I find out who dese cockaroaches are, they dead." He stomped his foot, like he was stomping on an imaginary bug. "They mothers are *dead* and anybody who know them—*dead!*"

"I got word out on the streets and I know that we'll know something soon," Lee assured his boss.

"Let it be known that I got a hundred thousand dollars for a name. All I need is a *name!*"

Lee nodded and said, "It's taken care of, Boss."

17

News You
Can Use

recious and Molly went out to lunch the next day. As they sat at the table, Precious listened to Molly go on and on about some of everybody's business.

She wasn't worried about Trill possibly being hurt or in jail, she was only concerned about where he was and whose arms he was in. Just when she thought Molly would never take a break her phone rang. She looked down at her Caller ID and saw that it was Trill. "Hey, baby," she said into the phone as if they were not on the outs.

"What's up?"

"I miss you, that's all."

"I bet."

"You miss me?"

"Look, I just called to let you know that I'm gon' pick up Lil' Trill from school."

"What? What made this come about?" Precious asked, surprised.

"He's my son."

"Okay, no problem," she said, knowing that Trill would have to bring Lil' Trill home and then they would get a chance to talk. This foolishness had been going on for too long.

"Aight," Trill said and then hung up.

Precious decided to put on a charade for Molly. "I love you, too, boo! But I love you more! See ya when you get home. Be safe, okay, boo?"

As Precious closed her cell phone, Molly spotted Tiffany. "Chile, there go Tiffany."

"Tiff, Tiff . . ." Molly waved to Tiffany. She winked at Precious and said, "Girl, let's get the scoop on this bitch." Molly flashed a fake smile at Tiffany; then, as the other woman made her way over, leaned in to Precious. "Girl, I heard that nigga Lee dissed the fuck out of her at the club and now she back in his face."

"For real?" Precious' miserable ass was now all of a sudden all ears, in need of company as she wallowed in her own misery.

Tiffany approached the booth, and Precious and Molly moved in closer so that she could join them.

"Hey, girl, sit down and join us," Molly said.

"I think I will," Tiffany said.

"That's a cute bag," Molly complimented Tiffany, knowing that she would get Tiffany's mouth going.

"Thank you." Tiffany blushed. "Lee bought this for me."

Precious tilted her glass up to her mouth to get some ice out of it. "Lee must be one of two things," Precious said as she crunched on the ice.

Both women looked at Precious in suspense.

"That nigga must really be crazy about you, or he must got money out the ass to give you that sixteen-hundred-dollar Chanel bag."

"Or both." Molly pumped Tiffany up, causing her to smile ear to ear.

Tiffany laughed. "Y'all crazy. He just got this for me because he ain't been spending no time because his boss been putting a bunch of pressure on him lately."

"Not that it's any of my business, but who is yo' nigga? And what do he do?" Precious knew who he was, but she wanted to get as much information on him as possible just in case she would have to get at him if Trill really left her.

"Girl, you know Lee, he works for that Cuban nigga, Diego. Since he started working for Diego, shit done been soo good. Money flowing like free cheese on the first."

"So, what's the problem?" Molly asked. "Don't tell me you tripping over some other bitch?"

"No. I have come to realize, a nigga like that, them type of cats, hustlers, they always gonna have more than one chick. As long as I get mines, I'm cool. Fuck it! It ain't even worth the stress no more."

"If it ain't no broad, then what is it?" Molly asked.

"His boss, Diego, is putting pressure on Lee to find out who these stick-up dudes are that keep killing and robbing his workers."

"I've been reading about that shit in the paper. Didn't they find a couple niggas dead in Sugar Bottom the other day?" Molly asked.

"Yup, the same guys stuck Lee up. Lee said that they were professionals, in and out, and didn't have a problem murkin' a nigga."

"How much they get?" Precious inquired curiously.

"I don't know," Tiffany said, shrugging. "But it was an asshole full. Enough to make Diego put out a reward."

"A reward?" Precious said, raising an eyebrow.

"Yeah, girl," Tiffany confirmed. "Diego told Lee to

put it out that he got a hundred thousand for anybody who can give a name of who's responsible. All he want is a name for a hundred thou."

Precious damn near pissed her pants.

"So whatever, they took, I'm sure it was big," Tiffany said.

"Excuse me a minute. I gotta go to the bathroom," Molly said.

"Me, too." Tiffany slid out behind her.

"You gotta go, Precious?" Molly asked her friend. Precious knew they were going to probably be talking about her in the bathroom but what the hell did she care? It wouldn't be the first time and wasn't gonna be the last.

"I'm good. I'ma stay here and watch the coats and bags," Precious assured the girls and waved them off to the bathroom.

Once they were out of sight, Precious dug into Tiffany's Chanel bag in search of her cell phone. When she found it, she went through the phone book looking for Lee's number. She got frustrated because she didn't see Lee's name anywhere.

"Shit, I know this ho got his number locked in," Precious said out loud, talking to herself. Then she saw an entry that read, "My Boo." *That's it. It gotta be.*

Precious tried to focus on remembering the number and after repeating it out loud a few times, she quickly put Tiffany's phone back where she got it. Before Tiffany and Molly returned from the bathroom, Precious had pulled out her own cell phone and saved Lee's number. Although in her heart she knew that the men Diego was looking for were Trill's, and there was no way she could bite off the hand that fed her, for some reason she wanted Lee's number at her fingertips for insurance. Just in case . . .

Daddy's Baby . . . Momma's Maybe

rill never brought Lil' Trill back home that night. Instead he dropped his son off at school that morning, and Precious was to pick him up. When Precious picked Lil' Trill up that evening she grilled Lil' Trill on the way home.

"Where did you and your daddy go?" Precious asked Lil' Trill.

"We had lots of fun," Lil' Trill said excitedly.

"Did you? What did y'all do?"

"He took me to Chuckie Cheese's."

"Where did y'all sleep last night?"

"At his other house." Lil' Trill changed the subject and asked, "Mommy, can you cook me some blueberry pancakes?" Precious nodded, distracted because she wanted more information. "And can you put a smiley face in whip cream on it tomorrow for breakfast before I go to school?"

"Yes, Lil' Stanley."

"Momma," he said, tapping her, "can you give me blueberry syrup, too?"

"Yes, I will." She raised her voice a little and then rolled her eyes. She thought for a minute and then asked, "Where did your dad take you for breakfast?"

"His friend cooked me breakfast."

"What's her name?" She moved in closer to him, but he knew better than to tell anything. Precious was mad.

"I don't know, Mommy."

Precious could tell that Lil' Trill had been coached on what to say and what not to say. As soon as she got home, she called Trill.

"Oh, you got bitches around my son now?" Precious fumed through the phone.

"What's wrong with that?" Trill asked.

"You got bitches cooking for him?" she cried. "I can't believe you would do something like this."

"I can't cook, so somebody had to," Trill said in a calm voice. "Precious, he gotta eat. Don't you know breakfast is the most important meal of the day?"

"So, you just parading bitches around my son, huh?"

DEATH BEFORE DISHONOR

She held the cordless phone to her ear as she walked back and forth hanging up new clothes in the closet.

"When I was in jail, didn't you have niggas around him? Huh? I can't hear you?" Trill pressed. "You act like you ain't never had no lame-ass niggas around my son." Precious was caught off guard. "You thought I didn't know?"

"What?" Tears crept from her eyes; she was in pieces, broke.

Trill knew it, too, so he kept pressing on. "Death Before Dishonor, huh? Guess that shit right there went out the window a long time ago. You forgot one thing, niggas talk."

"But Trill," she cried out in between sobs. "You can't believe these bitch-ass niggas."

"Save it," Trill shot back. "I know what the business is."

Precious' mind was all over the place. Her world seemed to be tumbling down in front of her eyes like the walls of Jericho. Though there were a million questions she needed to ask, first thing out of her mouth was, "So, are you gonna still maintain the bills here since I do have Lil' Trill here."

"About that, I'm home from prison now, I'll take care of my own son. But you can get visitation."

Nikki Turner

She felt like a doctor had just opened her chest cavity and was now squeezing the life out of her heart. Precious was left speechless.

"I got an important call on the other line. I'll hit you later," Trill said.

"Trill . . . more important than me?" she whined, trying to regain her composure.

"Right now a telemarketer calling would be more important than you."

He hung up the phone on her. Precious cried and cried until finally she pulled herself together and made a phone call.

"He knows everything," Precious informed the person on the other end of the phone. "I need to see you right away."

19

His!
Yours!
Mines!

ithin a matter of minutes, Precious' secret lover of seven years arrived at the house.

"He knows," Precious said to him as she paced back and forth.

"What the fuck you mean he knows?" he shouted.

"He knows," she echoed stressfully.

"How much?"

"He knows that I was fuckin' around while he was in jail and that I had the nigga around Lil' Trill," Precious answered.

"He don't know for real," he informed her. "That nigga was just bluffing."

"How do you know?" she asked nervously.

"Because if that nigga knew for sure, you wouldn't be talking to me right now, I'd be dead fo' sho'."

"I don't know," Precious said, biting her nails. "Trill is smart, he almost never reacts irrationally to anything."

"But this is different. He can be impulsive, too."

"Something's gotta give," Precious sighed.

Mont nodded in agreement and then asked, "Do you love him? Keep it real." She dropped her head and kept silent. "I mean, do you love him more than me?"

Precious shook her head and answered. "No," she said but it wasn't too convincing. "He's a good dude. Mont, I just had no idea that this would go on for this long. I thought I would just be setting him up in the beginning and then you and I would live happily ever after." Precious reflected back to that day of robbery. "But then I got shot and . . ."

"And that was that nigga's fault!" Mont spat, reminding her.

"I know, but then you"—she pointed to him, like she was picking him from a police lineup—"you wanted me to write him and stay close to him to make sure he didn't know you had anything to do with it."

"And, baby, you did just that," Mont said in a diplomatic voice. "You played your role perfectly, too," he assured her.

"Then . . . then . . . once he was in jail and started getting angry because his connect didn't get him a lawyer and he started talking 'bout getting niggas back and getting money on a higher level, you made me continue to play the part of loyal lover."

"And, baby, I am in debt to you for it." Mont rubbed the back of his hand gently down the side of Precious' face. "And when he was in jail, who took care of you?"

"You did," she said in a soft voice.

"He didn't have a pot to piss in or a window to throw it out."

Precious looked into Mont's eyes. "All in all, I believe he really cares for me. And if I needed to keep playing it out, I know I could. Deep down, I think he really loves me." Precious' eyes started to water.

"No, he don't," Mont snapped. "Don't you understand? He's given the new bitch something he's never given you."

"What might that be?"

"I ain't gon' front. That nigga has been loyal to you for years," Mont admitted. "When he got out, he could have rolled out on you, but he didn't. He got you a new leg, took care of all your medical bills, put you up in this house, filled the closets and the garage fo' you. But . . ." He laughed to put shit in the game. "But fucking you, to him, was like a chore. I never wanted to say anything to you, but he mentioned once that the thought of coming home to you and having sex turned his stomach." Mont lied to manipulate her.

Precious was crushed. Trill always seemed like he enjoyed their lovemaking.

Now that Mont finally had Precious where he wanted her, he went in for the kill. "And although he might've given you everything you could have ever wanted materially, there was something he never gave you."

"What?" Her voice cracked as she tried to hold the tears back.

Mont knew he had to make her see things his way so he could get her back under his command. "His heart," Mont answered her. "And that's where Sunni got you."

Precious tried to dress it up by rationalizing, "Well at least he's in debt to me, right? That nigga owes me. So I am going to always have one up on Sunni, right?" Precious started to second-guess herself.

"Do you know how he met her?"

"Out at that book-signing party."

"Nope." He shook his head and smiled. "He met her when he was on the run and she let him into her house. If those crackers would've caught him with all that coke they would have sent him away for life. So now, he feels indebted to her, too. After all, she saved him."

Although she didn't let on to Mont, that revelation blew Precious' mind. Standing there at a loss for words, Mont took her in his arms.

"Just a little bit longer," he comforted her, "then we can move away and live off of everything—his, yours and mines."

Mont knew he had convinced her to continue to play her role to the hilt. When he left, he was certain that Precious was back in his stable once and for all, just like she always had been.

Precious locked the door behind Mont and went and picked up her cell phone. She pulled up Lee's number and pushed send. While the phone rang and she waited for an answer, she said out loud to herself, "Correction, Mont, I'm gon' get yours, Trill's, Diego's and keep all mines." She laughed, while the song "Get Money" by Junior M.A.F.I.A. played in her head.

20

What's Beef?

"I'm about to cum! I'm cummin'," Trill yelled out, as he grabbed Sunni's hips and pulled them toward him. Upon hearing that Sunni threw her hips back and forth into it like never before. She wasn't about to let him get his off without her.

"I'm cummin' with you," Sunni moaned as her juices flowed down on Trill's stomach.

Trill smiled as Sunni collapsed on top of him.

After thirty minutes of laying in each other's arms, Sunni got up to use the bathroom, but never bothered to turn on the light. Just when she was about to flush the toilet, she heard Trill yell.

"What da? How da fuck did y'all get up in here?"

Trill screeched. He hoped that Sunni would be smart enough to hide or get out of the house.

"It's time to pay up," Lee said. "Where the fuck is yo' bitch?"

"She gone to work," Trill lied. "She left about an hour ago." Good thing Sunni's car wasn't outside. She had loaned it to Cher earlier that day.

"You kill my family, I kill your family," Diego chimed in with rage as smoke came through teeth that were clenching a cigar.

Hearing Diego's voice made Sunni cringe. Her first thought was to go out there shooting, but her gun was in the nightstand drawer.

"You kill my family, my workers, take my money and my drugs, you fucking cockaroach," Diego hissed, before putting his cigar out on Trill's leg.

"Aaahhg!" Trill yelled out as Diego twisted the burning cigar down deep into his flesh.

Diego then pulled out a pair of brass knuckles and hit Trill across the face, breaking his jaw.

"It's an eye for an eye," Diego said. "You can decide how long you live before I put you out your misery." Diego ordered Lee and the two other goons that were with him to beat Trill down with a crowbar.

"Where my money at?" Diego shouted.

"I don't know what you talking about," Trill moaned as blood seeped from the side of his mouth.

Lee started singing "Precious Lord, take my hand" before admitting, "Your ho told everything, but she didn't know where the money was."

Trill still didn't say anything. Sunni could tell that he was stunned by what Lee had just said. Sunni vowed, whether Trill lived or not, that she was going to make Precious pay.

The beatings continued but Trill took it like a man. As Sunni listened to the torture, tears flowed from her eyes. She wanted to cry out but she couldn't; her hands were invisibly tied and there was nothing she could do. She prayed that they wouldn't kill him. Now that she had finally found love, it was about to be snatched away from her. Agonizing pains shot through her stomach as she helplessly listened to her man tiptoe through the valley of the shadow of death.

"I got something that will make him talk, Boss." Lee smirked.

"Take him to the garage," Diego demanded. "Do what you have to do there."

Sunni felt like she was the one condemned to death. As they carried Trill to the garage, Diego grabbed a towel and Sunni's yellow mop bucket from out of the kitchen.

Diego pulled out his dick and pissed in the bucket and passed the bucket to everyone else to do the same.

"Where my money?" Diego asked.

"Boss, you want us to look around here?" Ricardo asked.

"No," Diego firmly answered with a clenched jaw before they all went into the garage, "he's gonna tell us."

Once Sunni knew they were in the garage, she quietly slipped on some sweats, a jacket and a pair of shoes. She grabbed Trill's cell phone along with hers. She crept out of the front door and then hauled ass to her neighbor's house but her neighbor wouldn't answer. Trill's cell phone rang, startling her. Noc-Noc's name showed up on the Caller ID. Trill had already introduced her to his cousin before. Sunni answered the phone and told Noc-Noc exactly what was going down.

Noc-Noc instructed Sunni not to call the police and swore that he'd take care of everything. He was in the area already, and would be over there in a few minutes.

"I love him so much," Sunni found herself saying to Noc-Noc. "I have to get him help. I have to!"

"I'm the closest to him and I promise you I'ma handle everything," Noc-Noc assured her.

"I have to call an ambulance to try to revive him," she cried, "I just have to."

"Okay, go ahead and call the ambulance, but listen, Sunni, you stay where you're at. These guys ain't playin' fair. Make the call and I'ma call you right back. Tell them that someone tried to rob your boyfriend. But don't go back near the house."

Sunni hung up with Noc-Noc and did just as he had told her to. She called from her cell phone as she stayed out of sight, hidden in the bushes.

In the garage, Diego and his team continued to torture Trill. They covered his mouth with a towel and poured the urine on it until it was totally saturated. Diego knew just how much time to leave it before it would start to fill Trill's lungs with the acrid liquid. Trill never uttered a word. Diego had Lee punch Trill in the stomach to stop him from drowning. It wasn't time for him to die just yet.

"You Americans." Diego laughed. "You Americans, you cockaroaches would die over pennies. You dumb. You have no honor."

"Suck my dick, you Jafakcan, banana-eating mother-fucker!" Trill managed to get out through his swollen mouth.

"Finish him off. Cut his vocal cords," Diego in-structed Lee, handing him a pearl-handled hunting knife.

Lee took the knife, looked to Diego, who gave him a confirmation nod, and then looked down at Trill.

Trill never begged for his life. Instead he stared Lee right in the eyes as he felt the blade cross his throat.

Once Sunni saw the Suburban shuttling Diego and his crew past her hiding spot, she ran back to the house. She was running as fast as she ever ran in her life. She saw Trill in her garage, lifeless. She ran over to him and cried with him in her arms.

"Oh God!" she cried out. "I love you, baby. I love you!"

She felt lifeless herself, as she sat with him. The thought of killing herself crossed her mind, like some ghetto Romeo and Juliet, but instead she screamed out, "Why him?"

It Ain't Over 'til the One-legged Lady Sings

recious had just gotten in from a full day of shopping when Noc-Noc called and informed her that his mother and sisters were in town and they wanted to see Lil' Trill. Precious didn't hesitate to let Noc-Noc come pick him up so that she could go back out and do a little more shopping.

When Noc-Noc arrived, ten minutes later, Precious greeted him at the door and invited him in. Noc-Noc's little sister took Lil' Trill to the car.

"You cool?" He came in and sat down, something he had never done before.

"I'm good. I just miss Trill, that's all." Precious hadn't heard about what happened to Trill, she thought he was staying away because he was still mad at her.

"I know. I ain't talk to that nigga in a couple of days myself. I've been laying low since that shit happened with dat nigga Seven."

"What happened?" she inquired, curious to know what Diego had done with the information she had given him.

"Seven locked up."

"What? Locked up? For what? What happened?" Precious asked, confused.

"Yup, he got bagged. For the past few weeks, he been fucked up. He been having these bad headaches," Noc-Noc confided in her like she was one of his boys. "Then he got shot about a week ago, and we took him to the best underground doctor money could buy. For some reason his wound got infected. He said fuck it and went to the hospital. They locked him slam the fuck up. So everybody been laying low. Shit is fucked up."

She shook her head. "Damn, now I am really worried about Trill. I really need to talk to him. I want him to get out of the game, so we can concentrate on my modeling agency."

"That's what's up. Me, I'm just gon' kick back with the family and live happily ever after," he said, standing. He looked at his watch, indicating that he was about to go. "What you 'bout to do since you kid-free?"

"Nothing much," she answered. "I'm tired, but I'm hungry."

"You should go get you something to eat."

"I am, I'll probably go to the Copper Grill or something."

"You got money?"

"Not really but I got enough to get me something to eat."

"I'll treat." He went in his pocket and gave her a hundred-dollar bill.

"Thank you." She was surprised because the only women who ever got money from Noc-Noc were his mother and sisters.

"It's nothing," he assured her, looking her in the eyes. "Take your time and be careful."

"I will," she said, trying to hide her smile.

"All right then," Noc-Noc said. "I gotta go pick up this rental, so I can take care of one last thing tonight." He gave her a brotherly hug. "If Trill calls, tell him to hit me up."

"I will," she said. After Noc-Noc left, she closed the door and locked it. Damn. She had gotten away with it. Hearing that Seven was locked up was music to her ears. It was only a matter of time before the police would have the whole crew imprisoned and she would be free.

Precious let out a laugh and sang "Bad" by Michael

Jackson and started dancing like she was in the "Beat It" video. She had her prosthetic leg going so fast no one would have known that it wasn't real.

Precious was on top of the world. Diego had doubled the reward money because thanks to Mont she was able to put a place with the name. She was sitting pretty as far as she was concerned. She had her own stash plus Mont was gonna take care of her just like he did before Trill ever came into the picture. It was the best insurance money any girl could have gotten without paying a premium every month.

She didn't know the outcome for Trill as of yet, but she did know that he wasn't answering any of his calls. Fuck 'em and feed 'em beans.

About a half hour after Noc-Noc had picked up Lil' Trill, Precious called Molly.

"Hey, girl, you want to meet for dinner?" Precious asked. "My treat."

"In that case," Molly replied, "hell yes."

"What are you in the mood for?"

"Umm, I don't know. What are you in the mood for?"

A huge grin came across Precious' face. "Lobster and steak . . . the best in town. I deserve it."

They decided to meet at the Copper Grill, and after taking a bubble bath and getting dressed in one of the outfits she had just purchased, Precious headed out the door. She had the music blasting in the Mercedes-Benz CL600 that Trill had bought for her. As she sat at the stoplight on Main Street, she never heard the tractor trailer approaching her—the vehicle that Noc-Noc had rented. The driver was going fifty-five miles an hour when it ran into the side of the Benz and dragged her car five blocks down the street, leaving Precious unconscious and staring death in the eye. At the impact, the airbags exploded to protect Precious from hurt or harm, but that was damn near impossible. Instead they just trapped her inside the crushed vehicle. The Starbucks coffee that Precious had gotten earlier that morning splattered across the interior of the car while the cup escaped out the window. Too bad Precious wasn't that lucky. The scraping sound of the metal dragging against the cement made sparks. The accident caused three more accidents.

She was rushed to St. Mary's Hospital. Once she was out of intensive care, she realized that her life, once again, had been spared.

"Where's my leg?" she asked the nurse.

"Ummm, I think it was left at the scene of the accident but don't worry, I'll help you fill out the paperwork so that the state can provide you with one."

"A state leg? Oh, hell no! I had the best leg money could buy."

"Well, maybe you can get one of your family members to go by the scene and see if it's out there."

The chaplain walked in and wanted to remind her that it was God's grace and mercy that saved her. After the chaplain said a prayer for Precious, he left her alone in her room to rest. Shortly thereafter, the nurse brought in a beautiful flower arrangement and a large brown envelope.

As the nurse set the flowers on the bedside table, she asked, "Would you like for me to read you the card?"

"Who else gonna read it?" Precious snapped at the nurse. The nurse looked at the card and didn't say a word. "What, you tongue-tied? Cat got your tongue?" Precious snapped.

The nurse cleared her throat and read the card out loud:

PAYBACK! PAYBACK!
I remember you from WAYBACK!
XOXO,
Death B4 Dishonor!

At the same time that the nurse was reading the card, Precious had opened the envelope which contained a sin-

DEATH BEFORE DISHONOR

gle picture: Mont staring wide-eyed at the camera, a bul-

lethole in his forehead. His tongue had been cut out of his mouth and was lying beside his corpse with the words "Death Before Dishonor" printed underneath.

Precious started to sob, because she knew she wasn't safe. Was it Diego who wanted to kill her because he knew she couldn't be trusted? Or worse? Could Trill still be alive? She knew she had violated in so many ways. She knew Trill's word was his bond. And she didn't want to face Trill's judgment day. Perhaps having her life spared by the mercy and grace of God was a curse more than a blessing. Only time would tell. She would have to wait, always looking over her shoulder, never knowing when she would take her last breath.

TURN THE PAGE FOR EXCERPTS
OF MORE G-UNIT BOOKS

from 50 Cent

BABY BROTHER

By 50 Cent
and Noire

Prison number: 837R2006
Height: six feet one inch
Face front.
(flash)
Turn to your left.
(flash)
Now to your right.
(flash)

ood morning, New York! It's time to get the hell outta bed! Right about now you're waking up with my girl Jonesy! Sure we hired her because she's pretty . . . but then after talking to her I realized she also has a great rap! Wake up on Hot 97! Let's get ta grinding on this hot, sunny morning in the Big Apple!"

The early-morning sun baked the rundown five-story tenement from the direction of Queens. On the second floor, thin red curtains swayed in the light breeze, and the B-20 to Spring Creek groaned toward Linden Boulevard, traces of its exhaust fumes wafting through the open window.

Inside the bedroom, Baby Brother plunged into his wet yummy, bumping bone and scraping walls. "Yeahhhh," he groaned, getting his mash on. He took a deep breath, then grunted and arched his back, pounding his pipe.

Beneath him, Sari moaned and panted. Her dark hair curled around her face and fanned over the pillow. Her juices smelled like Fruity Pebbles and it was just about breakfast time.

"Right there, Mami?" Veins bulging, Baby Brother demanded, flinging sweat. "Is that where you like it, baby? Right there?"

She tossed her head no, but still squealed in pleasure as he grabbed her toned thighs, spreading them apart in a wide V. His fingers were hot on her caramel-colored skin. She pulled him deeper into her, then whispered something nasty in Spanish as the headboard slammed against the wall and Miss Jonesy talked shit in the background.

"Cool," Baby Brother said, withdrawing until only the head was left inside. It pulsed and throbbed in the rim of her tight opening as he extended his arms and balanced himself on the palms of his hands. "If the dick ain't good to ya, then I might as well take it out."

She squeezed her legs tight. "No!"

He laughed. "Then let me hear you say this dick is good!"

"Sshh!" She stopped rolling her ass and frowned. "Why you gotta say 'dick' so loud like that! Tony might hear you!"

Baby Brother laughed again. "Fuck Tony."

Sari giggled and slapped his arm. Working her hips

into a hard-grind, she pulled him deeply into her soft gushy, then wrapped her long legs around his back as her teeth found his nipple. She swirled her wet tongue around his bud and sucked gently, her lips pressed firmly against the hard muscle of his chest.

Baby Brother clenched his jaw and shuddered. "Aaah, baby. Damn. Shit. Slow down. *Goddamn.* Slow down, Mami! Damn, you throwing some good-ass stuff around, girl."

It was sticky and hot inside her box, and he didn't wanna move. He forced himself to pull out of her, then slid down her body, sighing. He paused to lick her stiff, light-brown nipple, then continued south, lapping sweat from the crevice of her belly button before pressing his face deeply into her wet spot.

"Yummy . . ." he smacked between licks. Her juice was like honey. Sweet and thick, and he wished he could put his whole head up inside her.

Sari gasped. Her muscles went rigid as he made waves of pleasure flow from her center. She held tight to his head and opened her mouth. A Spanish pleasure tirade exploded from her lips and filled the whole room. "Aaah, baby! Yeah, just like that. Right there, just like that." Then moments later, "Oooweee, too deep! No, harder. Yeah. *Just like that!*" And then finally, "Oooh. Damn. Yeah. Damn! Why you gotta leave me, huh, Zabu? Why you gotta go? I love you, Z. You know that, don't you?"

Baby Brother moaned, spurting the last of himself into her warmth. He rolled onto his side and pulled her into his dark arms. He gazed into her flashing eyes, and despite the way their bodies had just battled, he saw the deep pain that was lurking there.

He kissed her damp curls and squeezed her closer. "I *gotta* go, girl. That's what's real. This ghetto's gonna kill me if I don't. But I'm coming back for you, Sari. That's truth, baby. That's truth."

Baby Brother stood up. He used a bunch of wet wipes to clean himself, then kissed Sari again and got dressed. It was time to go. Priest was waiting for him back at the crib, and they had moves to make.

"I'ma get up with you later, cool? I'll be waiting downstairs around six. Have your fine-ass ready too, 'cause the West Indian Day Parade draws niggahs from all over Brooklyn and there won't be no place to park near Eastern Parkway."

He winked at Sari, then walked over to the half-open window and raised it all the way up. He glanced down at the sparkling whip parked below, in the exact same condition he had left it in the night before. While her eyes were on him he pretended he was climbing out the window and onto the raggedy fire escape, but then turned around real fast and walked over to the door instead. He heard her shocked intake of breath as he reached for the knob.

"Z! What the hell you doing?" She jumped up with her eyes flashing with alarm. He liked it when she got all hyped. Her nature was a perfect indicator of her ethnic mix. Black and Hispanic. She was a down chick and had a temper on her, too. "Don't open that damn door! You gotta go out the window!" She snatched the sheet off the bed and tried to wrap it around her nakedness. "Man, Tony's home! You can't let him see you leaving outta my room!"

Baby Brother grinned and walked out, closing the door on her high-pitched protests. Fuck all that window action. He was leaving out the door today.

His light-brown eyes danced and his skin looked chocolatey smooth against the red-and-white Rocawear shirt he wore. He hiked up his jeans until they settled over his Air Force Ones just the right way, then headed down the short hall toward the front door.

Passing the kitchen, he stuck his head inside, then slammed his hand against the side of the refrigerator as hard as he could. A cracking sound exploded in the air, startling the handsome Puerto Rican killer sitting at the table. Out of nowhere, a small silver gat appeared in the man's hand.

"Damn, Tony! What? You gone shoot me, or something?"

Tony stared at him with a snarl and set the gun down on the chair between his thighs. Even in the heat his voice came out feeling like ice.

"Yo, muthafucka. What the fuck is you doin' in my crib?"

Baby Brother checked out Sari's half-brother. Sari's father had been black, and while she was brown and curly-haired, her brother Tony was a pale Hispanic with dark, piercing eyes. He'd been sitting alone in the kitchen smoking a dutchey and counting a large stack of chips.

His jet-black hair was shower-wet, his bare chest stained with tattoos and bulging with jailhouse muscle. A large baggie half-filled with white powder sat on the table in front of him, and another much smaller bag rested on a triple-beam scale.

"Damn. Whatever happened to 'Good morning,' man?"

Tony pushed the stack of money aside and reached into his back pocket. The glint of his knife caught Baby Brother's eye.

"Yo. You been up in my joint all night?" His voice was deadly. "Back there witcha dick up in my little sister?" He twirled his knife. The tip of his blunt glared red, and his cold eyes never left Baby Brother's face. "You must be a bad motherfucker then, huh?"

Baby Brother laughed and held up his hands. "Chill, *amigo*. I ain't the enemy, man. Shit, after three years I'm just about family. Plus, I'm about to be outtie in a minute. No disrespect to your crib or nothing. I just wanted to spend some time with Sari. You know, treat her right before I leave, man."

Tony stopped twirling the knife. Baby Brother knew how sharp that blade was. Tony was almost as legendary as the Monster had been on the knife tip. Both of them had plenty of carved-up victims walking the streets.

"That's right, I forgot. You graduated. Now you runnin' off to college to be some kinda fuckin' professor or something." He laughed coldly. "That's real stupid, yo. You need to claim you some territory and be a real man now, homey. You can fuck my little sister in my crib, then come stand in my kitchen where I can smell your nuts? Yeah, you a fuckin' man. But real men pay dues, amigo! Leave that college business for the herbs out in Canarsie and get yourself a grind. Business is good on this side of the bridge. Tell ya pretty-ass brothers you coming to work for me now."

"Man, what I look like? You can kill all that shit. I got plans. I ain't slinging rock for nobody. Not for you, not for that stupid nigga Borne, and not for my brothers neither."

Tony laughed. "Okay, okay, I tell you what! I'm a nice guy. Those fuckin' twins can come work for me too, cool? You can be my runner, and your brothers can be my capos. You can hold my balls, while they take turns suckin' my dick!"

Tony laughed louder this time, sweeping half the bills off the table and to the floor as he gripped his knife in his fist and glared.

Baby Brother watched him for a moment, then walked toward the door shaking his head. Tony had been tryna get at him for years, but it was cool. He was the oldest boy in the Santiago family, and Sari was the youngest and only girl. It was only right that he would look out for his little sister the same way the six older Davis brothers came to the table for him.

Baby Brother and Sari had been rolling together since he was in the tenth grade and she was in the ninth. They were on opposite sides of a family rivalry. The Davis twins, Farad and Finesse, controlled the rock and the powder flowing in and out of Brownsville and were well-known for their savage brutality. The Santos clan ran the streets of East New York, with Tony at the helm. He was ruthless and crazy. A cutter. Like the Monster. A loose missile just itching to launch. There was no love lost between the two families, but they tolerated each other. Mainly on account of business, and partly because of Baby Brother and Sari.

Baby Brother walked down the hall and went through the stairwell door. The hot smell of stale urine and beer rushed out at him. He maneuvered around a couple of winos and crackheads who were sitting on the stairs trying to come down off their all-night highs.

"Whassup, Felix. Big Porter. How you doin' this morning, Mrs. Woodson?"

The woman he addressed beamed at him. She was Jelly's moms, a dude he knew from way back in the day. They'd boxed together at the BBC gym, but Jelly had gone into the Marine Corps two years ago, and it wasn't long after that that the streets had claimed his mother.

"Baby Brother!" the woman exclaimed. She pulled her bra strap up on her shoulder and tried to smooth her hair. "You almost ready to leave us, huh?" She nudged the crackhead sitting next to her. "This boy right here is something else. He used to be Jelly's best friend, you know. He was the only kid who ever whupped my Jelly in the ring, too. Now he's going off to college to learn how to be an astronaut! Ain't that right, Baby Brother?"

He smiled down at her. Her hair was raggedy and her teeth looked like rotten little worms, but Baby Brother showed her much respect.

"Nah, Mrs. Woodson. I'm gonna be a surgeon. I'm majoring in pre-med." The odors assaulting him were excruciatingly foul, but he withstood them. He stood there and carried on a conversation with Mrs. Woodson the same way he used to when his boy Jelly had still been around. He talked to her the way he used to talk to her back when she was still a loud-mouthed, heavyset, dark-skinned woman holding her family down in a cool apartment off of New Lots Avenue and pushing a decent whip. As cracked-out as Mrs. Woodson was now, and as dreadful as she smelled, Baby Brother treated her the same way he would've wanted somebody to treat his own mother if he'd had one.

"Boy, you got a future ahead of you," Jelly's moms told him. "A real future. Wherever you goin' to school, hurr'up and get there. This place ain't for boys like you. Don't let it crush you like it done crushed me."

Baby Brother stepped out of the building and into the hazy sunshine. He inhaled the morning air and gazed at the candy-red 2007 drop-top Mercedes parked at the curb. The whip was just like he'd left it, and he wasn't surprised. Everybody in Central Brooklyn knew Farad's wheels when they saw them, and only a fool with a death wish would have laid a finger on the paint.

"Baby Brother!"

His name rang out from a doorway across the street.

"You tell that niggah Farad his g-ride ain't as tight as mine!"

Baby Brother grinned and lifted his chin at the skinny

brother standing on the stoop. It was Bip, one of Farad's
ex-partners. A guy who had grown up with the Davis
brothers in Brownsville but who slummed around in East
New York now. Bip had been banned from Brownsville on
the direct word of Farad. He'd been allowed to keep his life
because they'd been dawgs damn near from the cradle, but
even that wouldn't stop Farad from having him murked if
he got caught crossing over into The Ville.

"That's truth, Bip. I'ma let him know that shit too."

"Yeah. Let him know I been up watching his whip all
night, yo. Tell him he owe me! If it wasn't for me, some
base-head prolly woulda ran off with his spinners."

Baby Brother unlocked the car and climbed behind the
wheel. It was a quality ride, paid for with cash dollars.
Farad had it detailed every three days, and it smelled fac-
tory-fresh at all times. He settled into the seat, then slid
the key into the ignition and listened to the engine purr.

He drove down the streets of East New York with the
top down, driving aimlessly and absorbing the hood vibe.
N.J.S. beats blared from the speakers as Reem Raw killed
a hot track with illa New York lyrics. He rode up Shepherd,
crossed Linden Boulevard, and headed toward New Lots. It
was early, but niggas was already out on the hot streets
scheming on their next hustle.

Baby Brother nodded at a few familiar faces as he
cruised down the block. He stopped at a light on the corner of Hegeman Avenue. A couple of gansta-looking niggas with larceny in their eyes grilled him as they walked
by. Baby Brother was up on them. He knew what they
were thinking and hoped they were smart enough to think

again. He was a hard nigga, and good with his hands. He'd come up on the streets in the gym, trained by his brothers to get in close and handle his.

But with two days left in New York he wasn't trying to get into nothing hot except some more of Sari's yummy. He pumped the volume even higher and decided to let Farad's whip speak loud and clear to anybody who might wanna get smoked.

On the way home he thought a lot about college and about Sari, too. Leaving her was gonna be hard, but he knew it would pay off in the end. A degree from Stanford came with certain guarantees, and although he was gonna miss the comfort of having his brothers around, he was grateful for the opportunity to escape the urban jungle. It's what their mother would have wanted. Their father, too.

Pulling over at a corner candy store beneath the Number 3 El, Baby Brother went inside and bought a soda and a bag of pretzels. When he came back out a bunch of kids were admiring Farad's whip. He let them climb inside and blow the horn and push a few buttons and shit, then he got behind the wheel again and made his way back to The Ville, where his brothers waited.

$\mathcal{P}$riest had just finished his breakfast of buttery grits and eggs when the front door slammed. Three of Farad's soldiers were posted outside, and relief flooded Priest as he heard familiar footsteps approaching. Baby Brother had stayed in East New York all night long, and even though the kid was eighteen now, he still worried about him, especially out there messing around with them treacherous Puerto Ricans.

"Zabu!" he called out, his voice heavy and full of bass. "You late, man. I told you I was gone take you to get some suitcases today, but if you wanna haul your gear to Cali in some black garbage bags, you can do that, you know."

Despite his bark, Priest's eyes were full of pride as his youngest brother strolled into the kitchen. Just like his six brothers, Baby Brother was tall, with deep mahogany skin and amber eyes. He was muscled up and perfectly cut, and although they all worked out hard, the majestic physique was just part of their genetics.

Priest was the oldest son and the most battle-scarred. He had raised Baby Brother and the other boys after their mother died, and Baby Brother was his heart. His favorite. His salvation. Priest couldn't help it. These days he served as an assistant pastor of a small storefront church, operated his own barbershop up on Rockaway Avenue, and gave Bible lessons at a youth center twice a week.

But he had a past that just couldn't be wiped clean. He had pimped women, slung rock, slumped foes, organized gangs, and hustled the hell outta the game. But looking at Baby Brother killed all those past demons. His little brother was his pride and joy. Hard evidence that despite all the grimy capers Priest had pulled, all prey he'd bitten, and all the upstate prison time he'd served, that somehow God had favored him and allowed him to redeem himself and do something right. Every time he looked at Baby Brother, Priest saw the man that he himself should have been.

"What it do, 'Twan," Baby Brother gave him some dap on his way to the refrigerator.

"You late, man. I told you we was leaving at nine."

Baby Brother flashed him a grin and rubbed his stomach. "I'm hungry, tho'. Gotta stick something in my belly before we roll."

Priest opened the microwave and took out one of four plates he'd covered in Saran Wrap. "Here." He set it on the table. "Put ya face in this and hurry up. I gotta be back for services this afternoon."

"Aiight. Yo, why's it so quiet in here? Where is everybody?"

Priest shrugged. "You know the scene, man. When you do your work under the dark of night, you gotta regroup when it's light. The twins are both upstairs. Matter fact, Malik's gone be here in a minute. Go upstairs and tell them two knuckleheads to get down here and eat."

Ten minutes later Priest sat at the head of the table watching four of his young brothers grub. Malik had arrived dressed in his NYPD blues, and as they dug into the plates he'd prepared for them, Priest couldn't help but smile inside. It felt good to sit at the same table with his cats. Raheem had taken a trip for the long weekend, and Kadir was down in the A.C. doing his thing, but with Baby Brother leaving for college in a couple of days, both of them would be showing up to see him off.

"Snatch 'em!" Malik hollered real loud.

"Guard ya plate!" Baby Brother threw his arms on the table, encircling his breakfast with wary eyes.

"Man, keep your hands off my damn food!" Farad complained, setting his fork down. "I ain't playin that 'snatch 'em' shit today, dawg. You betta chill with that."

Malik laughed and stuck the stolen slice of turkey bacon in his mouth. "You ain't gotta play nothing but defense, man. You know the rules, muhfuckah! Lose ya heat, I snatch ya meat!" Laughter rang out around the table, and Farad reacted quickly.

"Snatch 'em!"

Finesse cursed as his twin snatched a crisp slice of bacon off his plate and started crunching.

"You getting slow, nigga," Farad chuckled. "I coulda got me two pieces off you, yo."

Priest laughed along with them, but his heart was heavy. He had prayed for a better life for his brothers. Nothing would make him happier than seeing Farad and Finesse out of the game and doing something legitimate with their skills. He'd dreamed of opening a chain of barbershops and installing one of his brothers at the helm of each operation, but Raheem and Malik both had good jobs with benefits, Kadir was hooked on card tables, and neither of the twins was interested in a nine-to-five. Priest stood up and refilled Baby Brother's glass from a container of juice on the counter.

"So," he said, looking around the table before nodding at his youngest brother. "Everybody 'bout ready to get rid of this lil' cat? Ain't but two days left, then he's out."

Finesse shrugged. "I'd rather see him bounce for a minute than have him scrambling yay like them niggas on the stoop. Shit, B-Brother. You gone be on some real West Coast shit when you get back. You sure you can't go to school somewhere in New York? Maybe upstate?"

"I can go almost anywhere I wanna go," Baby Brother said. "But Stanford is giving up the best scholarship package, man. Plus it's a top school. I'd be crazy to let something like this slide by me."

Malik nodded, wiping his mouth. "That's what's real, man. Graduate from Stanford with a degree in shit shoveling, and you still considered a heavyweight in the corporate world. Fuck around with one of these city schools, and you might end up working for Transit or coming on the force, or worse—following Ra down to Corrections and getting on over there." He tossed his plate in the trash. "Cali is a good bet for you. Go for it. We got your back."

"Yeah," Farad said, standing up with his empty plate in his hand. He reached over and punched Baby Brother on his shoulder, then mushed his head like he was ten years old again. "Just make sure you put some damn gas in my car before you fly, though. Shit! I'm glad that nigga leaving. I'ma finally get a chance to push my own whip."

Malik headed for the door. "Yo, Ant, what time we flying outta here on Monday?"

"Seven. I already told Ra to be here by four. That'll put us at JFK way before five."

"Cool." Malik nodded. "I'll get wit'chall in a few. They got me pulling a double shift, so it's gonna be a long night."

Fifteen minutes later two of the Davis brothers were ready to hit downtown Brooklyn. Priest let Baby Brother drive. He couldn't bring himself to get behind the wheel of Farad's drug-bought car. Negativity was all up in it, and he wanted no part of that.

THE SKI MASK WAY

By 50 Cent and K. Elliott

he fruit punch–red Impala had gold Dayton rims. The car gleamed so much, you could see your reflection in the hood. The interior was cream-colored leather. The car had been totally restored. The Impala was the only one that Butter owned and he cherished it. He and Seven sat on the hood of his car, smoking purple haze, listening to Mobb Deep's "Shook Ones Part I."

"This was my shit back in the day and those niggas was from round my way," Seven said.

Butter puffed the blunt. "You knew them?"

Seven reached for the blunt. "Well, not exactly. My manz in'nem used to hang with Prodigy; but, naw, I ain't know them, but I seen them a few times."

"I listen to them, when I'm about to do a lick, you know?" Butter pulled out a .380 and cocked the hammer. "It gets my adrenaline going, you know?"

"Man, put that gun away," Seven said.

"What, nigga? You scared of guns? How the fuck is

you from New York and you afraid of guns?"

"Naw; I ain't afraid of guns—just high, careless niggas with guns."

Butter put the gun on safety.

"I didn't know niggas in the South was into that Mobb Deep shit."

Butter looked confused. He didn't say anything, he just puffed. Finally he couldn't control his thoughts or his tongue.

"You know what? Y'all New York niggas always think that we slow down here. I can relate to Mobb Deep."

"I feel ya," Seven said. "Calm down, son. I mean, I ain't mean it like that." Seven did think southern niggas were slow, once upon a time, before he'd gone to Virginia. He'd met some real gangsters in Virginia. Butter seemed to be through. He'd met him at a temp agency where they both were applying for a job and started talking. After a fifteen-minute conversation he realized they had a lot in common: They both were street niggas and ex-cons.

"So what you're all-time favorite gangster movie?"

"Dead Presidents."

"I expected you to say *King of New York, New Jack City, Menace II Society.* Never did I expect you to say this."

Butter inhaled the haze and then coughed. "Yeah, I liked that movie."

"I liked *Paid in Full,* myself" Seven said.

Butter coughed again "Yeah, that shit was crazy; those mufukas was making a lot of money."

"You know what my favorite scene was?"

"What?"

"You know the scene where Mitch calls Rico and tells him he has coke and Rico flips and kills his man for the work?"

"Why is that your favorite scene?" Butter asked.

"Because the lesson learned is niggas will kill you for life-changing money. My daddy always told me two things: Your friends will kill you for the right price, and every bad guy likes to think of himself as good," Seven said.

"Was you and your pops smoking weed when he told you that shit? Sounds like that weed philosophy," Butter commented.

"That's real talk, man, from a man who's doing life in the pen."

"That's why you gotta watch everybody." Butter blew out a huge smoke ring, pulled the gun out, cocked it again, then kissed the barrel. "I'm 'bout hit a lick tonight, man. I needs some money in a major way."

"I ain't got shit myself, and that motherfuckin' baby mama is nagging the shit out of me. My son is two and can't walk—he needs physical therapy. The bitch ain't got no insurance." Seven thought about his boy and other problems he was having. He hardly ever had money. Sometimes he would detail cars for hustlers but he didn't have any real paper—not like he was used to—hell, before he'd gotten locked up he had thousands of dollars on him at all times. Now it was down to this petty assed car washing—he felt like a sucker.

Butter sat back on the Impala. Young Jeezy was now coming from the Chevy. "You know what? I thought you were locked up three years ago in Virginia. Right."

"Yeah."

"How the fuck did you get her pregnant, anyway? I mean, I was thinking about that shit one night. I was high as fuck, sitting outside, looking up at the sky and shit. You know that's when you high; you have the strangest thoughts."

"Now that's got to be a weed-induced thought."

"I was on that purple haze and my mind was just racing and shit, and I was thinking of all kinds of stupid shit."

"Well, Adrian was actually a guard that I met while I was on the inside. I started banging her and the warden got wind of it. Fired her and put me in solitary confinement," Seven said.

Butter's eyes grew wide. "Nigga, quit lying."

"I'm serious. One thing about me, man, is that I've never had a problem with the ladies, I've always been able to pull them." Seven was indeed a ladies' man. Very attractive dark smooth skin, wavy hair; his body was well-defined and his teeth were eggshell white. The women loved him.

"Damn, that's an amazing story." Butter said.

"Yeah, man. That's how the shit went down. I got her pregnant. We kept in touch while I was in prison and she moved to Charlotte, N.C., so that's why I relocated here."

"Why did you relocate here?"

Seven inhaled the blunt. "Damn, nigga, you a news

reporter? Motherfucker, why so many questions—you the FBI or something?"

"Naw, just making sure you ain't FBI," Butter replied.

"I mean I got three sisters and three brothers in New York, but I ain't really fucking with them like that. I mean, the whole time I was down only one of my sisters came to visit me so I ain't really have no reason to go back to New York and I ain't going back to Virginia cuz all my niggas locked up."

"Damn. You came all the way down here not knowing anybody."

"I wasn't afraid. The only thing I was worried about was that bitch tripping, and she tripped and put me out. But, it's okay, I got my own room in the boardinghouse and I got some pussy, so I'm good."

"Nigga, you must not be used to having money."

"Now that's where you're wrong at. I made a lot of money. Ran with a fucking crew—and most of them niggas that I ran with are either dead or in jail."

Butter rolled another blunt, lit it and inhaled, then blew another smoke ring before coughing loudly.

"What the fuck were y'all doing?"

"Coke, heroin, e-pills . . . all types shit."

"I can't believe that shit, man, cuz it just seems like you are so content with being a average motherfucker."

"Nigga, you average," Seven said.

"But I ain't never got no real money, nigga. I bet y'all seen millions."

Seven thought back. A few years ago he was driving Porsches, BMWs and shit with expensive rims. Ever since he'd been released from prison a year ago, it had only been a bus pass. He really wanted money, too, but he didn't know anybody who would give him drugs. He was in Charlotte. Nobody knew him. This was both good and bad. It was good because he didn't have a reputation to keep, but it was bad because he couldn't get anybody in Charlotte to supply him.

Butter passed Seven the gun. "Got this motherfucker for two rocks, nigga, it was brand-new in the box."

"What you mean you got it for two rocks, you ain't no hustler."

"I know but I have drugs because I'm the type of motherfucker that takes shit from the dope boyz, you know, if they making money I'm making money because they have to give me money or else I'll rob they punk ass. I actually took the dope from a nigga, gave it to another motherfucker for the gun and when I got the gun I robbed the nigga that sold me the gun and got my rocks back . . . that's how ya boy Butter gets down."

Seven laughed but he really didn't think that was funny. He'd been around niggas like Butter before and knew he could only trust him as far as he could see him.

"So—do you want to help me with this lick?"

"So, who is this cat, Caesar? And does he have money?"

"He has a Colombian plug, and word in the street is he gets those bricks for thirteen five. He just bought this stripper bitch a Benz for her birthday."

"How can we get at him?" Seven wanted to know. He remembered the days when he was dealing in Richmond, Virginia. He knew that the streets talk, especially in the south; news spread like wildfire. Things that were just ordinary conversation could be made into major news. He also knew that whoever Caesar was, it wasn't going to be easy to get to him.

"One thing you have to always remember is that most of these major drug dealers are cowards. You don't have to worry about them. It's the niggas around them that you have to worry about; the enforcer-type niggas. Those are the hungry mufuckas that will do something to you," Butter pointed out.

"Exactly. I know this. I mean I ain't never stuck nobody up, but I know the fuckin' streets. I know legendary stickup kids in New York. I'm talking about kidnap-your-mom type niggas, son."

Butter chuckled to himself. He never understood why New Yorkers called everybody "son." A motherfucker could be seventy years old and still be called son.

"I know what ya mean. But—back to the business. You with me or not?"

Seven thought for a moment and took a puff of the blunt. He knew that if what Butter said was true, he would be doing a lot better than he had been doing. Hell. He lived in a boardinghouse with twelve other sweaty men and one crackhead woman. He wanted out of that place more than he did prison. He envisioned taking kilos of coke from the drug dealer with the Colombian connection. "Yeah. I'm down, son."

Butter tossed him a pair of gloves and a ski mask and a sawed-off pump shotgun. "Let's get that money the fast way the ski mask way."

"The ski mask way. . . . Hell yeah." Seven said. He and Butter high-fived.

The subdivision was called Peaceful Oaks. A quiet neighborhood in the southeastern part of Charlotte. It was predominantely white, which meant they had to be very cautious. White people called the police at the slightest bit of suspicion. Two black men rolling through suburbia after midnight was not a good look. Butter and Seven rolled through the neighborhood looking out for Good Samaritans—people that wanted to be on the news saying that they tipped the police.

Caesar's street was Peaceful Way Drive. Butter went one street over, to Peaceful Pine Drive, and parked the car in the driveway of an abandoned house. He and Seven hopped over the privacy fence in the backyard into Caesar's backyard and looked around, but didn't see anybody. Then Seven saw the sign that read ADP in front of the door.

"He has an alarm. Man. What do we do about that?"

"He has a baby, too."

Seven looked confused. "What the fuck does that have to do with anything?"

"Don't worry about this shit. I've done it before. I got this player."

Seven put on the mask and the gloves. He thought about prison; the sick old men there, the perverts, the liars and the snitches. He didn't want to go back to that place. They went around front. Nobody noticed them and the street was dark.

"On the count of three, I'm going to kick in the door.

I want you to go in one room and I go in the other, just in case there is somebody else in the house."

"Nigga, you've done this shit before for real?" Seven said.

Butter's face hardened. "This ain't no fuckin' game to me, man. I need to eat."

"Okay. Let's do it."

Butter kicked the door in and ran into the first bedroom.

Seven ran into the second bedroom and found a man and a woman on the floor, naked. He pointed the gun at the man. "Okay, I need you to get the fuck up and your bitch to stay on the floor with her hands on her head."

The man was shaking and it looked as if tears were in his eyes. *Damn, what a bitch-assed nigga,* Seven thought.

"Nobody is going to get hurt as long as long as you do what the fuck I say."

Butter walked into the room with a little boy wearing Elmo pajamas.

"Look what I have."

The little boy began to cry

The alarm went off. Caesar said, "The police will be here soon. You don't want to go to jail, do you?"

Seven said sarcastically, "Yeah. That what we came here for . . . to get caught and go to jail." He slapped Caesar with the barrel of the gun.

"Don't you say a motherfuckin' thing."

He walked Caesar into the hallway to the alarm keypad.

"Disarm the alarm," Seven ordered.

Caesar punched in the code.

The telephone rang. Butter picked it up without answering it. The caller ID said ADP.

"The fuckin' alarm company."

"Well, we knew they had an alarm," Seven said.

"Don't worry," Butter said, and he walked the phone over to Caesar with the infant still in his hand, crying. "Tell them everything is okay," Butter said, "If you try some slick shit, I'll blow your fucking block off, nigga."

"Hello," Caesar said.

A female voice said, "This is ADP. Is everything okay?"

"Yes, everything is fine. I just didn't get to the alarm pad on time."

"Okay. What is your password."

"My password?"

Butter clenched his teeth.

"Tell the bitch your password or else it's going to be a fuckin' bloodbath in this motherfucker. I promise you, man."

"The password is *rubber.*"

The little boy started crying louder.

"Okay, sir. Are you sure everything is okay?"

"Yes; everything is fine, ma'am."

"Do I hear a child crying?"

"That's my son. The alarm scared him."

"Okay, sir. You have a good night."

Butter snatched the phone out of Caesar's hand and terminated the call.

"Okay, man. Where the fuck is the dope, nigga?"

"Ain't no dope here, man."

"Okay, motherfucker. You think I'm stupid?" Seven said through clenched teeth. "You think I believe you *worked* for this house and that fat-assed Benz you got outside? You think that I think this fine-assed bitch is with you for you good looks?" Seven looked at the female, who was still facedown and shaking nervously.

"Where the fuck is the cash?" Butter said.

"I'm telling you I ain't got shit."

"Nigga, you ain't gonna have no fuckin' son if you don't give us what we want."

"Please don't hurt my baby," the woman said, then stood.

Seven pointed the gun at her.

"Bitch, get back on the floor."

"Where the fuck is the dope?" Butter repeated.

"There ain't no dope here."

Butter walked over to the window and pulled the curtains back. "I'ma count to three. If you don't give me some dope or some money, this little boy is going out of the window."

"Put the child down," Seven said as he thought about his own little boy. He never had a soft spot for kids until he had brought Tracey into the world.

He and Butter made eye contact before Butter said, "Nigga, you don' tell me what the fuck to do. I'm telling this motherfucker if I don't get what the fuck I want, this little boy is going out of the window."

The woman stood and Seven aimed the gun at her again. "Get your ass back on the floor."

"No. Please, please don't hurt my baby. I'll tell you where the money is."

Seven cocked the hammer of the gun. "Well, tell me where the godamned money is, then."

"Please, put my son down first."

Butter put the child on the bed.

The woman went into the closet and pulled out a large green gym bag. Butter unzipped the bag and saw bundles of money. He zipped the bag back up.

"Okay; where's the dope, bitch?"

"There really ain't no dope in here. I swear to God," the woman said.

"Okay."

Butter stepped out of the closet.

"Bring him to me," Butter said to Seven.

Seven walked Caesar over.

"Okay, nigga. Where ya fucking car keys at, and ya guns and shit?"

The woman got the keys from the nightstand and handed them to Butter.

Butter duct-taped Caesar's hands and feet together and handcuffed the woman to the bed.

The baby was still crying. Seven walked over to him, ran his fingers through the toddler's hair and said, "It's going to be okay."

They left with the money.